Reports on the Internet Apocalypse

Also by Wayne Gladstone

Notes from the Internet Apocalypse

Agents of the Internet Apocalypse

Reports on the Internet Apocalypse

Wayne Gladstone

Thomas Dunne Books
St. Martin's Press
New York

THOMAS DUNNE BOOKS.
An imprint of St. Martin's Press.

REPORTS ON THE INTERNET APOCALYPSE. Copyright © 2016 by Wayne Gladstone. All rights reserved. Printed in the United States of America. For information, address St. Martin's Press, 175 Fifth Avenue, New York, N.Y. 10010.

www.thomasdunnebooks.com
www.stmartins.com

Designed by Steven Seighman

Library of Congress Cataloging-in-Publication Data

Names: Gladstone, Wayne, author.
Title: Reports on the internet apocalypse / Wayne Gladstone.
Description: First Edition. | New York : Thomas Dunne Books, St. Martin's Press, 2016. | Series: The internet apocalypse trilogy ; 3
Identifiers: LCCN 2016016413| ISBN 9781250048400 (hardback) | ISBN 9781466849266 (e-book)
Subjects: LCSH: Internet—Fiction. | BISAC: FICTION / Literary. | FICTION / Humorous. | FICTION / Technological. | GSAFD: Satire. | Humorous fiction. | Dystopias.
Classification: LCC PS3607.L3436 R47 2016 | DDC 813/.6—dc23
LC record available at https://lccn.loc.gov/2016016413

Our books may be purchased in bulk for promotional, educational, or business use. Please contact your local bookseller or the Macmillan Corporate and Premium Sales Department at 1-800-221-7945, extension 5442, or by e-mail at Macmillan-SpecialMarkets@macmillan.com.

First Edition: November 2016

10 9 8 7 6 5 4 3 2 1

This book is dedicated to the first Starman, and everyone still brave enough to look out their window for another.

Prologue

My name is Special Agent Aaron N. Rowsdower. Or at least it used to be. I served at the Federal Bureau of Investigation for over twenty years, and I was a good agent. After all that time, I could tell you some stories, but that's not what I do best. I solve puzzles and fix problems. I investigate.

A little over a year ago, I was just another agent doing everything I was supposed to do, even if I wasn't where I should have been. Then the Internet Apocalypse came and the NSA followed. I thought that might be my ticket. A way to help me get noticed by someone in Washington. So, yeah, I was a willing foot soldier of that bullshit NET Recovery Act, tracking down leads that went nowhere, harassing people who told me nothing, but I wasn't hurting anybody. Not really. The bosses were pleased. Keep it up, they said. This will be good for you.

And that's when I met Gladstone. I say that like it was

some big day, but it wasn't. As far as I was concerned, he was just a sick, sad man. Someone claiming to be the Internet Messiah, or at least that was the claim some made about him. But I'd seen his file. I saw his divorce and psychiatric disability from the New York Workers' Compensation Board. To me, he was nothing more than everything that had failed about Generation X. A broken man, flailing hopelessly at the new millennium. I had no idea how important he would become to me in the months that followed. To everyone. And I certainly didn't know he'd bring me to Los Angeles. Something I still can't forgive him for.

Before Gladstone, I had a destination. Or at least a plan. Maybe that's not true either, but I did have a job. I was relieved of my duties shortly after his release from custody. Not that it was Gladstone's fault really, but if not for him, I'd still be at the FBI right now. I'd be a whole other man. So, no, I'm not really Special Agent Rowsdower. It's just Rowsdower now. Aaron N.

What follows are my reports on the Internet Apocalypse. My attempts to find Gladstone and all that followed. This is a story about how a search for one man gave us a chance to reclaim not just the most significant technology of the twenty-first century, but everything we'd lost.

Part I

Report 1

I didn't want to go back to L.A. Just being there made me feel like a willing part of a global conspiracy. A perpetual fraud selling the lie that a bunch of suburbs connected only by traffic and false kindness could qualify as a city. But I had a lead. Someone who had seen Gladstone after the shit went down. When he was on the run from the same men who will no doubt come for me.

So I went back west. Back to a place where every bartender and waitress calls in sick whenever *CSI* holds an audition. Where they ask if you'd prefer whites only when ordering scrambled eggs with toast. But at least this woman I was trailing didn't travel in the usual L.A. circles. After three days of shadowing, I hadn't seen one yoga class or spa visit.

I followed her to the market at Laurel Canyon and watched her sit outside, sipping coffee while she wrote. I'm not sure what she was working on. It could have been a screenplay or just some bills. Maybe she was writing letters. There was no ostentatious MacBook display. The point was just to take care of business, and it seemed she liked doing it among other people. I saw her compliment absolute strangers on their clothing. Unexpected gestures of kindness that in New York might make you take a step back and double-check your wallet, but I'd watched her long enough to know she wasn't crazy.

Whether hiking in Will Rogers State Park or window-shopping in Santa Monica along Main Street, she seemed to navigate the world under the false belief that no one would take notice. She was wrong. She stood five-ten easy, and looked taller because her legs went on forever. Her fingers were long too, and her face was slim and elegant, but set above shoulders and hips too broad for her to be some French supermodel dying of consumption.

It seemed like as good a time as any to make contact. Besides, it was raining. At least in West Hollywood, where she'd brought me. I stepped under a black-and-white awning on Santa Monica Boulevard and lit a cigarette, watching her scurry unprepared along the wall of a sound studio on the other side of the street. She stopped for a moment, knowing she'd have to make a decision before the rain turned her white blouse translucent. And as striking as that visual was, I was distracted by the graffiti of Gladstone's Net Reclamation Movement along the high-ceilinged studio wall in the distance. It was the Wi-Fi symbol wearing an M-shaped fedora, but this one had a more ominous message than the one outside the Veterans' Affairs Building, where I last worked. That one had read, THE INTERNET IS PEOPLE AND WE'RE STILL HERE.

But this was done in black paint, dripping with anger: THE INTERNET IS OURS AND WE WANT IT BACK.

She turned in my direction, but she wasn't looking at me; she was heading to the dive bar/restaurant I was standing in front of. The Formosa Cafe. She crossed the street, stopping under the awning for a moment to push her fingers through her short blond hair, and flipped the excess water at my feet before entering. It would have felt like a rebuke for smoking so close to a public building, but she looked like she wanted a drag herself. I let her go inside and kept smoking. I only allow myself three cigarettes a day, and I wasn't going to waste this one. Besides, she wasn't going anywhere in this rain.

Inside, she was sitting on a barstool, legs crossed, dripping over her vodka or gin. She was set apart from the China-red shadows only by a reflected light shining off the photographs above. A string of autographed celebrities hanging in black and white, smiling for the cameras of a different time. Ghosts of success either keeping guard or bearing witness.

I sat down at the stool next to her and flagged the bartender. Except for some geriatric drinking his medicine at the end of the bar and a twentysomething fiddling with the antenna of an old Sony Watchman in the window, we were the only ones in the place.

"There's a whole bar," she said, and poked at her already-drowned lime.

"That's true, but I'm not here for the Shanghai rice cakes," I said, referencing an appetizer placard on the counter. "I'm Aaron Rowsdower, formerly of the NET Recovery Act Special Task Force and Federal Bureau of Investigation. I'd like to ask you a few questions."

The bartender came over. He was pushing thirty. Strong jaw. Blond, with just a hint of carefully manufactured curl. He still had dreams of saving the next "It" girl from invading aliens in a summer blockbuster.

"None for him," she said. "He's on the job." The bartender looked to me for confirmation before she continued. "Speaking of that, shouldn't you be showing me a badge or something?"

"There's no badge for being a former agent, Ms. Zmena," I said, and turned to the bartender. "Johnnie Walker, neat, please."

She took a sip from her drink, trying not to appear alarmed that I knew her name or as if she already knew mine. But I'd worked this job for twenty years. I knew what the appearance of indifference meant. She tilted her glass and stopped the ice with her teeth, letting the liquor slide underneath. Then she took one cube between her molars and crushed it. "Tell me," she said, after the damage was done, "are people usually willing to talk to men without a badge?"

"I don't know," I said, and placed a twenty on the bar. "I'm new to this."

Now I was the one lying. I remembered my last badgeless interrogation from weeks before. Back in Perth, all I needed was $100 Australian to get Ozzygrrl69 to tell me what she knew. Oz, real name Melody Andrews, was that former webcam girl Gladstone kept some online company with before the Net went down. She was also the one he imagined as a companion, stumbling through New York, drunk and alone, purportedly looking for the Internet. I had a hunch, only a hunch, that when things fell apart and Gladstone had to run away to the farthest point from his existence, he'd seek her out. Some men can't heal without women, and I knew Gladstone was one of them. It was clear to anyone who read his journal. And while I in no way believed he'd murdered his ex-wife, I also knew he'd run out of women. Scared and alone in a strange country, it was hard to think of him going anywhere but to Oz.

I'd started tracking her down back in America while I was still on the job. Back when I'd reviewed that ballistics report on Beth "Romaya" Petralia that made no sense. Judging by the damage done, the trajectory of that fatal bullet had to have come from above, not—as the story went—her estranged husband standing one foot away. And just when I started asking questions, Romaya's body was cremated with seemingly no request to do so. I started to suspect that this broken man had somehow staggered his way into importance. And if not importance, then he'd made the wrong people uncomfortable. Something I'd avoided my whole career. At least until the very end.

So I found out Ozzygrrl69's real name and all it took was getting on the phone and threatening an internationally sanctioned subpoena. It didn't matter that I couldn't imagine what such a document would look like. I was speaking with an entire government behind me then, and Australian online sex syndicates already had enough trouble with the Apocalypse, plus giant killer spiders. They didn't need more grief. I got her name and found her working in a massage parlor on James Street, above the Sssh Shop and Phero-moans—two sex stores that connected with an adjoining door. I was out of my element, but it was good to know that just like

Americans, Aussies liked their smut infused with stupid sex puns.

I'd followed her from home to work and even paid for what I imagined would be a happy ending rubdown. I wanted to talk, and I wasn't afraid of being mistaken for the kind of man who paid for sex in a country on the other side of the world. I went to the room the peroxide blonde at the front desk told me to, pointing my way with fake red fingernails pressed into fleshy, nicotine-stained fingertips. I sat in the chair waiting. Smoking.

Oz entered a few minutes later, acne visible through too much foundation. Her hair was black and tightly androgynous, and tats had begun crowding her arms, revealing a haphazard use of limited space. But her eyes were big and blue, and when she spoke there was a brisk coarseness cut by an almost imperceptible lisp.

"You're supposed to be on the table, hon," she said.

"I'm here to talk to you about Gladstone."

"Who's that?"

"The dark-haired, five-foot-seven American you called a customer back in the Internet days. The same crazy man, reeking of Scotch, who came to see you a few weeks ago."

I could tell my hunch was right. I felt bad that a woman in her line of work had lost the distance of the Internet to keep her safe when she had no poker face. But I also had a job to do, even if I was no longer getting paid for it. Even if my efforts were only for my own self-preservation. It was time to finish this off.

"The man wanted for the murder of his ex-wife."

"He's wanted for murder?" she asked, and I felt almost guilty about how easy this was.

"He surely is," I said, disguising that no part of me wanted to slander Gladstone for that. I'd seen killers. Sat across from them. As a young agent, I was part of a team that hauled a child murderer out of the suburbs and into the back of a car. I've heard men order hits over the phone. I've tracked the emails of men in suits, ending lives as easily as purchasing stock and for the same goal of making money.

But I also watched Gladstone for over a month. I watched him eat. I watched him break down. I watched him hold on to tiny shreds of his dignity, cobbling pieces of himself together over and over until they resembled the shape of a man. And he did it all knowing they'd be blown down again. I could call Gladstone many unpleasant things: delusional, arrogant, irritating, ineffectual but I couldn't call him a murderer. Even without those bullshit ballistics and cremation reports. Even without the neighbors I interviewed who said they'd heard a helicopter the day Romaya was shot. I had sat with Gladstone and I knew my suspects. But the big murder display got Oz talking. What she knew anyway.

"Yeah, he came to see me, but I know fuck-all about murder. He just kept calling me Oz and babbling about the Internet, and some name. Rome? Something weird."

"Romaya?" I offered.

"Yeah, that's it. Fuck kind of name is that?"

"His ex-wife's. Now deceased."

"Yeah, well that's it. Wanted me to go off with him. Run away."

"Why didn't you?"

"Because he was babbling nonsense. He scared me. And he was broke."

"Did you remember him from the Internet?" I asked.

"No."

"Did you tell him that?"

"No."

"Good," I said. "He's suffered enough." I stood up and put a hundred dollars in her hand before leaving. "Anything else you can tell me?" I asked, and she grabbed her purse to hide the money as quickly as possible.

"Um, would this be helpful?" she asked, pulling out a business card. "Another American came looking for Gladstone a few days after he saw me."

The business card read PRAGUE ROCK PRODUCTIONS, MARGO ZMENA, OWNER/CEO.

The bartender returned with my Johnnie Walker and took my twenty. I tried to stare at Margo in a way that would get her attention, but failed. "I just got back from Australia," I said. "Ever been?"

"I have," she said, realizing there'd be no point in lying about something I already knew. Instead, she changed the subject. "Didn't anyone ever tell you it's bad manners to wear your hat indoors?"

"Oh, this?" I said, removing the fedora and placing it on the bar to the left of my drink. "It's not mine."

"Whose is it?"

"I think you know that, Ms. Zmena."

The bartender dropped eleven bucks' change on the bar. A five and six ones. He was no dummy. I pushed two forward, and Margo spoke up. "Another vodka soda please, Harry," she said. "This one's on him."

"Ms. Zmena, you don't have to talk to me. You're smart enough to know that. So why don't I just tell you what I think I've already figured out. And maybe if you're impressed enough with my detective work, and you like me enough as a person, and the liquor's good enough, you'll reward me with some honesty."

"Sure," she said. "And don't worry. If I'm not impressed, I'll just blame the alcohol to spare your feelings."

"The hat belongs to Wayne Gladstone, and according to his journal, his grandfather before him. But as I said, you know that. You know that because you've read his journal. As an L.A. resident, you were probably one of the first to read his *Notes from the Internet Apocalypse* when it took off. In fact, I wouldn't be surprised if you even attended one of his Messiah Meetings at the Hash Tag, where he first assembled the Net Reclamation Movement in an effort, somehow, to find a group of people to return the Internet."

She recrossed her legs and I did my best not to notice, because I'm sure she felt hungry eyes all the time. "How'm I doing?" I asked.

"One second," she said, and took a sip of her new vodka and soda. "Well, so far the alcohol's fine."

"Fair enough, Ms. Zmena," I said. "So anyway, here you are. Thirty-five years old, starting your own production company—I'm a little iffy on that part—and here comes a story about an Internet Apocalypse and a would-be Internet Messiah. I'm guessing you went to Australia to option the rights to Gladstone's story. I'm not sure where your money's coming from, but I think you sunk it in Gladstone for a score."

Just then the twentysomething in the window seat started complaining. He wasn't pleased with the Kung Pao Chicken.

"What's this?" he asked the waiter, pointing to a very specific part of his plate.

"Bean sprouts," the waiter replied.

He grabbed the menu. "Show me," he said. "See? Chicken, onions, red pepper, peanuts. Where does it say bean sprouts?"

"They're on top? Would you like me just to remove them?"

"Forget it."

"I'm sorry, sir," the waiter said.

"I just should have been warned," he said, and segregated the sprouts from the rest of his experience as the waiter returned to the kitchen.

Margo used the interruption as an opportunity to shift focus. "Is that really Gladstone's hat?" she asked.

"I found it at the LAX lost and found, and the blood I had cleaned from it matched his late ex-wife's, so odds are good."

"Why didn't the police have it as evidence?"

"Yeah, why didn't the police have it as evidence? And why don't I work for the FBI anymore?"

She ran her long fingers around the end of the brim, pretending there was something to discover by touch. "You think Gladstone was set up?" she asked.

"Yes."

She still didn't trust me enough to speak. But she had a tell. Her trust revealed itself with a slight tilt of the head. Like the curve of her tiny smile even if her lips seemed to stay straight and silent. I could see her comparing me to the predatory animal Gladstone had unfairly portrayed me as in his journal.

"And what about these bombs going off? Think he has anything to do with that?"

Things had started exploding after Gladstone's journal went paper viral. First figuratively, with photocopies being passed around from person to person, and the sketch drawing of a Wi-Fi symbol wearing an M-shaped fedora on the book's cover page popping up as graffiti—especially with FREE THE MESSIAH written under it while he was in captivity under the NET Recovery Act. But things started blowing up literally after we let him out. People had died. Senseless acts of terrorism, and usually accompanied by the Messiah symbol. The dead ex-wife was only one part of what sent him running.

"I've not seen one thing about Gladstone, in terms of evil intent or even organizational skills, that would lead me to believe he has either the desire or the ability to cause that kind of destruction."

It was the perfect thing to say to Margo, and it had the added benefit of being true. She titled her head. "Anyway," I continued, "I got your card from a lovely Australian named Melody Andrews. Y'know . . . Oz?"

"Yes, I met Melody," she said, fully aware she still hadn't told me anything I didn't already know.

"May I ask how you found her?"

She laughed. "Really? After all that, that's the part that's stumped you?"

I downed my drink and flagged Harry for another, swapping my card for the bills on the counter.

"You're blushing," she said.

"Must be the booze. I get red sometimes."

"Y'know," she said with an actual smile, "I think Gladstone was way too hard on you in his journal."

"I know, right?" I laughed. That's how she conceded all my hunches were correct. In the form of an almost compliment.

"So, Former Agent Rowsdower," she said, "buy me one more drink and I'll let you call me Margo. I've always hated the way 'Ms. Zmena' sounds like 'misdemeanor,' and coming off your lips, it's especially bad."

"OK, Margo." I waved at Harry, pointing to Margo's empty glass. "I'm Aaron."

"How do you think I found Oz?" she asked. "She's a prostitute. I offered money. Just posted a bunch of 'have you seen this man' postings around the shadier parts of Perth and she found me."

"And how did you know to go to Australia?"

"Same as you, I suppose. I'd read his book. Where else would he go?"

"And you bought the rights to his story?"

"I did."

"How much?"

"Enough for him to get away. Start a life. He had nothing. It would have been very easy to take advantage of him, but I didn't."

"And you won't tell me where to find him?"

"I don't know. He has my card if he needs to contact me, but I don't know where he's gone or what he'll do."

"One more question," I said, and she waited. "The weather said thunderstorms all day. Why didn't you bring an umbrella?"

"Why didn't you?"

"I had a hat."

"Well, I never use them," she said, but then downed her drink and added, "people who use umbrellas are always the last to know when it's stopped raining."

I would have tipped my hat, but it wasn't mine, and it was already resting on the bar. I would have done a lot of things, but that's when an explosion went off. It was so big it shook us from our stools, blowing out all the windows. Car alarms pierced even the ringing in my ears. From my knees, I saw the twentysomething on the floor. He wasn't moving, and Margo was trying to stand, pressing her fingers just below her collarbone, blood spreading through her blouse like a marker held against paper.

Report 2

Maybe Harry had a future as an action hero after all, because he stood up looking impossibly well coiffed and rugged. The geriatric at the end of the bar seemed OK too, stumbling around and getting back on his stool with no signs of bleeding. I rushed over to Margo.

"Let me see," I said, but she didn't move her hand from the wound. "It's OK," I said, and worked my bulky fingers over hers, gently pulling them from her chest. I hold the length of her hand in my fist. Her wound dripped, but didn't squirt. That was a good sign. Seemed like she'd only caught a shard of glass from the exploded window. The picky eater in the booth didn't fare nearly as well. He'd caught the brunt of the window, unwittingly taking one for the team. A sacrifice he never knew he made, and he was gone before anyone could say thank you.

"Call 911," I shouted to Harry, and hurried outside to get a better idea of what happened.

Across the street, most of the sound stage was now gone. At least, the parts I'd seen before. The remaining wall had what was left of the Messiah symbol, with fire spitting from the black smoke rising behind it.

"Bullshit," Margo said, pressing a few bar napkins against her chest.

"What are you doing here?" I asked. "Get back in there and wait for the ambulance."

"Oh, right away, sir," she said. "I'd salute you, but I'm afraid it might upset the old war wound here."

"Exactly. You're bleeding. Wait for the ambulance."

"Gladstone didn't do this," she said.

"How do you know?" I asked. "I thought you only met him once."

"You think he did it?"

"No. I told you that already, but we'll talk about this *after* the ambulance comes."

"Well, you're a man of action," she said. "Surely you can get me to a hospital."

Margo rode shotgun, holding the slowly filling napkin to her chest as I drove to Cedars-Sinai.

"So this is what FBI drives," she said.

"No, dollface, this isn't my G-ride. It's just a stupid Nissan Altima I rented."

"Did you just call me 'dollface'?" she asked, and I laughed, positive that a certain percentage of her offense was feigned.

"Too much?" I asked.

"Just warn me before you say it again so I can take off this napkin and bleed out first."

"Fair enough," I said, and handed her my hanky. "Looks like your napkin's had it."

"A hanky?" she asked. "Did you just drive through a wormhole from the 1940s?"

I ignored her question. "So is this a good time to tell me where your money comes from?" I asked.

Maybe it was because I'd passed enough tests to be trusted. Or maybe it was because I was looking after her, but Margo started talking. And although her speech was still immaculately controlled, there was also a sense of relief, like a diligent employee finally getting a well-deserved vacation. It felt good to be that comfort for her.

Margo Zmena graduated from the University of Michigan, and went to L.A. after college, brought there by a boyfriend turned husband. By my guess, he was the first person smart enough to get her jokes. But even a loner like me knows that's not enough, and when the laughter ended, she was stuck there. Not really stuck, because she somehow learned to like it. Love it even. She learned the back roads to the highways that kept me in traffic. She found the hole-in-the-wall takeaways while I struggled with main-strip dining. She made L.A. her home and she did it at the right hand of C. Martin Rubinek, or "Marty," as she called him during our drive.

"Why do I know that name?" I asked.

"Because he was a big fucking deal in Hollywood for over fifty years?" she offered.

Seems Marty never snitched during the Red Scare, and although it didn't get the press, apparently, he called Joseph McCarthy a dirty son of a bitch a full two years before Chief Counsel Welch did that whole "no sense of decency" thing. A big splash, forgotten to history. He swung too early to be safe and it finished him, for a few years at least. He went to New York, found work in theatre, and got to come home eventually, because, as he apparently liked to say, he took enough abuse without dying. Margo paused for a moment when she told that part. It was something she admired, and I wondered what wreckage she'd crawled from.

Marty started Phoenix Pictures in 1960 when he was still young enough to work too hard. Or maybe that had nothing to do with it, because even fifty years later, in his early eighties, he was still running a profitable production company. Margo was proud of her time with the last remnant of Old Hollywood.

"Why'd you leave him?" I asked as we sat waiting in the emergency room, and all that pride dissolved.

"You think I should have stayed a personal assistant forever?" she asked, turning to notice the rush of new patients flooding in. We'd come right in the middle of the ambulance brigade, and dozens were in greater need than she.

"If you liked it," I said. "But no, I guess you don't seem the personal assistant type."

A tiny part she forgot to hide was flattered. "I was young," she said. "I needed a job. I kind of loved it, and staying there also made me uncomfortable."

There was a TV in the waiting room. It wasn't just L.A. There were more attacks. Explosions in New York at the Kmart in Penn Station, and in Florida at Disney World. This was coordinated violence, strategic death, and all within spitting distance of Gladstone's Wi-Fi symbol each time.

"Jesus fucking Christ," I said, and Margo flinched, unsure she was still sitting next to the same man who believed in Gladstone's innocence. I wondered too.

"I'm going to find whoever did this," I said, trading anger for resolve.

She pressed her wound, watching the damage being done to the world. She saw the fire and wailing, all the increasingly familiar signs of tragedy. I watched her watch them. My hanky filling with her blood.

When you're an investigator you learn there are all sorts of ways to ask questions. Some get answers, but sometimes getting answers isn't the point. Sometimes it's just about fucking shit up. Disturbing the waters. You never get a clear picture looking through a splash, but sometimes motion reveals a trace of what's been hidden.

"I'll ask you again," I said. "Where's Gladstone?"

"Oh, *there's* the Rowsdower from the journal," she said. It was meant to hurt me, and it did. "So now you think it's Gladstone again? I gave you my answer. I haven't seen him since I bought the rights to his journal."

"Not even an option?" I asked. "You bought the rights straight out without even a studio behind you?"

"It's a good investment. Marty would have approved," she said, and that's when I understood.

"Oh, it's Marty's money."

"No," she said, really angry this time. "Marty's dead. It's my money. But he was a very kind man. I wasn't even his assistant when he passed."

"Just how kind was he?"

"Is that your business?"

"Enough to retire?" I asked. It was the right question.

"Maybe if I were fifty-five instead of thirty-five," she said.

"But enough money to quit the day job and start your own business?"

"Right."

"OK, Margo," I said. "I got it now. You quit your job with Marty, floundered around with, I don't know, copywriting, and . . ."

"Branding," she interrupted.

"Whatever. And then Marty dies, gives you a bunch of money, and you decide to start Prague Rock productions. You spot Gladstone's story. You watch him speak at one of his Messiah Meetings at the Hash Tag, and when the shit hits the fan, you seek him out in Australia and buy the rights to his journal. Swinging for the fences, in one fell swoop, instead of starting with a bunch of smaller projects."

"Well, I can hardly produce a web series right now, right?" she asked.

"Did I get it all right, Margo?" I said.

"You did," she said. "Even the part about seeing Gladstone at the Hash Tag. How'd you know that?"

"Because this is what I do."

"Well, you're a very good agent."

"Not anymore. You can thank your buddy Gladstone for that. How much money did you give him again?"

"I told you. Enough to get settled and start over, but not a ton. A girl's got to eat."

We turned back to the breaking news on the hospital TV because I suppose it was easier to look at the people dying on a screen instead of those around us.

Even with shock close-ups of covered bodies dissolving into long shots of smoke and tears. All of it happening in the shadow of Gladstone's symbol. It was a strong mark to be sure.

CNN cut back to the studio and suddenly there was a guest via satellite. Hamilton Burke, the billionaire Gladstone claimed to have met. I wasn't sure if that had happened, but it seemed a strange thing to invent. Burke was wearing one of his omnipresent three-piece suits that he'd sported on the cover of so many money magazines in the '80s. His hair was combed straight back like Nixon's, but gray.

Anderson Cooper was conducting the interview from his desk in a navy-blue suit that shined in the studio lights. "Mr. Burke," he said, "you recently had some harsh words for this administration. Would you care to explain?"

"Anderson," he said, "this isn't about taking pot shots at the president. Now is a time for action, and I'm sure this administration is committed to finding those responsible for these grievous and unspeakable acts."

"So, do you retract your quoted comments from earlier this week where you expressed frustration with the president's failure to return the Internet to full capacity?"

"Not at all, Anderson. I was voicing the frustration of the people. I mean, this is an administration that took months to get its health-care website working right? The private sector would never accept such results. You don't get to be on top without demanding performance, and the American people deserve such action."

My hanky was now soaked and I wondered if seeing Burke had quickened Margo's pulse. She was paler, but seemingly due to anger rather than blood loss.

"Not a fan of Mr. Burke? I thought you had a thing for rich old men?"

"If you truly thought that, then I take back everything I said about you being a good agent."

"I'm sorry," I said. "That was shitty. Did Gladstone mention Burke to you?"

Margo didn't answer. She just pressed my hanky harder against her chest.

"Tell you what," I said. "Why don't you tell me where to find Gladstone so he can tell me himself?"

"I've already explained. I don't know where he is."

She was getting tired, and it seemed a good time to push. I had to be an agent first, even without a badge. "Bullshit," I said, and this time I managed to surprise her. "I went looking for you before you ever came home. You went to Australia before I did and came home way after."

"I was on vacation." Her head tilted slightly.

"And?" I asked.

"And I met a boy," she said. "Is that a crime?"

"Who?"

"Don't worry," she said. "He's just a miner, not an Internet Messiah."

Just then, a nurse called Margo's name and she stood with her eyes on me. I wasn't sure what she was waiting for, but I didn't give it, and she returned my bloody hanky.

"Thank you," she said.

"You're welcome."

She paused a moment longer. "It was a pleasure to get to know you, Special Agent Rowsdower."

"Aaron," I said.

"Thank you for the ride too," she said, and meant it. She also meant it when she said, "I'll take a cab home," before following the nurse for her stitches.

Letter to Margo Zmena from Parker Lawrence

Dear Margo,

The day after you left, I ran out of shaving cream, so I soaped up my face and I shaved without it. That's how I realized I don't really need shaving cream. And when I ran out of whiskey, I didn't buy more, and that was OK too. Then I weaned myself off coffee. It really only took me a week to start living like a monk. Asleep by 10 and up by 5. I've already dropped five pounds.

And then there's the job. I've been working like a bastard. It's mindless and hard and that's good too. I drive the trucks and gather what needs gathering. I get the minerals from point A to B. I eat when they tell me to eat and work when they tell me the time for eating is over. It's nice to be told what to do for once. I try to be a good employee, and I try not to think of you.

It took me a while to realize that's what this was all about. You were a beautiful distraction, but I'm too tired of needing things that go away. I'm not trying to make you feel guilty. You've done nothing wrong, I'm just tell-ing you where I'm at. It was good to have you for the *time I did even if I cringe in embarrassment thinking of how I was. You deserve a full man.*

Love,
Parker

Letter to Parker Lawrence from Margo Zmena

Dear Parker,
You are a very silly boy. Do you know that? In fact, I think you're the silliest boy I've ever known. What does it even mean to say I "left"? Yes, you are there and I am here, but we've only just met. You know where to find me and I know where to find you.

If I need a man who eats as fast as he thinks, I know where to find you.

If I need someone dark and strong, with skin that seems always in shadow, I know where to find you.

If I need to feel the strength of a miner's hands on me, a solid mass against my body, making me feel both protected and possessed, I know where to find you.

If I need to be held gently all through the night by someone who'll never let me go, even reaching out for me through sleep, I know where to find you.

If I need someone brilliant who is too sure of himself and filled with too much doubt, I know where to find you.

If I need a man, I know where to find you. And if I need a boy, I know where to find you because you are also a boy. The best boy, and I'm so lucky you like me.

Love,
Margo

Letter to Margo from Parker

Dear Margo,

I keep thinking about the weeks we played house. Me going off to work, you turning my little apartment into a home while I was away. It was the happiest I've been in a long time, but I have to confess, I totally fucked up all your Feng Shui in these last few weeks. I pulled the mattress off the bed and dragged it into the living room. It looks terrible, but it helps me not miss you. When I slept in the bedroom, all I could see was you not being there.

During those first sleepless nights I missed the Net like I haven't for months, because I hoped it could bridge the distance. I could Skype you and watch you sleep, or you could watch over me as I slept. But even if the Net were back, it wouldn't work. Not with the time difference. I'm up when you're down. I'm at work while you're sleeping, and I don't know what to do because I'm not so sure I can live without you as easily as shaving cream or various beverages. (I know, the sweetest, right?)

Did I ever tell you that I think of you as an older woman? I mean older than I am. But before you get annoyed, you should know that in my mind, I'm still about twenty-five so you're still your age. Anyway, I don't know what it is, but you look like my childhood memories of grown women. The ladies in magazine ads or the cover of board games. I'd stare at those women and wonder who they were. The words they'd say if they were real and could speak. And now I think I know. You are my child's conception of a grown-up dynamite lady.

And this is all my way of saying, I know it's a big trip, but can I see you again? Can you come back before I destroy this apartment further? I don't want to end up sleeping in the tub.

I miss you.
Love,
Parker

Letter to Parker from Margo

Dear Parker,
Playing house was so much fun. And I realize now I didn't say something I should have before. I know you're not at your best now, but you are stronger than you know. That's all for now, Parker, because I'm on my way to the airport.

Love,
Margo

P.S. I'm on my way to see some dumb boy in Australia.

Report 3

After that first meeting with Margo, something changed. She wasn't like Oz. Back in Australia, it made no difference that I didn't have a badge. Oz crumbled under questioning like any frightened civilian, but Margo kept her fear double-wrapped and out of view. That was fine. I didn't want her to be afraid, but I wasn't prepared for how she looked at me. I thought she saw a man without a job. I felt ashamed and out of place, and when I returned to my case file it no longer seemed like a collection of reports. Just a pathetic way to pretend I still had a foot in my old life. But in time, I saw things more clearly. In the shadows of the Formosa Cafe, Margo's eyes seemed brown at first glance, but flecks of green emerged if you looked closer. After a few days, I realized the shame I saw was only my reflection. If I stared through that sheen there was a trace of curiosity. And why not? She was seeing something uncommon. A free man.

These reports were not just an excuse but part of a story I wanted to tell. Sure, twenty years in the FBI had trained the way I write and think, but this wasn't just business or pretend business. I had to admit I wanted this to be read, and in that way I was far worse than Gladstone. He just recorded his journal full of fractured thoughts in real time and let it reach the world by accident when his gossip-blogging cohort Brendan Tobey spread photocopies without his involvement. But I wanted to be heard. So Gladstone held the status of noble poet fuck-up and I was just an asshole trying too hard.

But once I admitted what I was doing, I started revising the reports. Moved things around a bit to help me tell the story. I need the help. I'm not like Gladstone. All my life I've stared at the finish line, and let the running take care of itself. Others wallowed in the moment, but maybe in that wallowing they noticed things I had not.

When you have no new leads, you go back to the old ones and turn them over to see if anything's grown during your time away. That's why I went back to Professor Kevin Leonards. I'd met him briefly in my final days wearing the badge, based on information I got from Tobey, who was behind bars with a psychic named Jeeves. They were awaiting trial for allegedly helping Gladstone blow up the Hollywood sign. I didn't believe that charge any more than I believed Gladstone had shot his ex, but while I had Tobey in custody, I tried to get some information. But for a slacker stoner, he had a pretty impressive resolve, keeping his answers terse while living inside a quiet calm He hadn't broken yet, and it wasn't my place to break him. Not just because I thought he was innocent but because I was on a different case. I knew the men who had jailed him would soon be coming for me. They'd be coming for anyone who asked too many questions or knew too much. Anyone who'd spent too much time with Gladstone. The best thing I could do for Tobey was to find them first. But every question I asked, he twisted into something sexual and stupid. It's not worth repeating what he said after I made the mistake of saying I wasn't going to be too hard on him. You get the idea.

So aside from taking some potshots at Gladstone, whom he still blamed for his predicament, all he told me was that they'd gone to visit Professor Leonards of UCLA shortly before things got messy. Some called Leonards the father of the Internet, but every successful child has more than one father. I went to him, but I was still a member of the bureau at the time, still a reminder of the NET Recovery Act, and he'd disliked me instantly.

"Oh, Special Agent Rowsdower," he said, repeating my title with more disdain than I thought justified. "Are you here to detain me indefinitely under your NET Recovery Act?" he asked, and offered his wrists right there in the doorway of his home on Thayer Avenue. Ordinarily, I would have said something like "I hope that won't be necessary," but there was nothing to be gained from that here. Bullying would only push him further into the position of dissident activist, and I could tell it was a role he'd enjoy too much. "I'm not here in my official capacity, sir," I said. "I don't have a warrant or anything."

"Warrant?" He laughed. "You know as well as I do that your NET Recovery Act requires no warrant for persons of interest, isn't that right, Special Agent Rowsdower?"

I had insisted that Gladstone address me by my full title, but on Leonard's lips the words felt degrading. "I wish everyone would stop calling it *my* NET Recovery Act," I said. "It's not mine."

"Just following orders, huh?"

He'd gone too far. I wasn't a scholar of Internet culture, but even I knew once you brought up Nazis, you'd lost. "Professor, I have no desire to threaten you, so I'd appreciate it if you'd stop trying to goad me into doing so. I'm here because of Gladstone. May I come in?"

"Wait a second," he said, remembering something. "Rowsdower. Aren't you the guy from Gladstone's journal?"

"Goddammit," I said. "Is there *anyone* in this city who hasn't read that piece-of-crap diary?"

"He was kind of rough on you," Leonards said. "Your teeth look normal to me."

"I know, right? And a yellow laminated skull? What'd I do to him?"

"You mean besides hold him for questioning with zero Constitutional mandate?"

"Well, yeah."

I laughed at myself, and that bought me some credit with Leonards. He took a step back to size me up again. Much of the contempt had waned, but not nearly enough trust or interest had taken its place.

"I'm sorry, but it seems being old has made me brave. If you want in, you're gonna have to be the bad guy you insist you're not," he said, and closed the door.

Based on that encounter, there was little reason to believe he'd be happier to see me several months later, but I had something else going for me now. I was unemployed, and that was a good thing, because in my time away it seemed he'd become even further entrenched. He now had a placard on his front lawn of Gladstone's Wi-Fi symbol, along with the message I'd seen before: THE INTERNET IS PEOPLE. AND WE'RE STILL HERE. It seemed the bombings couldn't damage this message that was too incongruous to the violence.

He came to the door with even more confidence and composure than he had in the months before.

"Special Agent Rowsdower," he said. "What brings you here this fine June morning?" I began to speak, but he interrupted me. "You got a new hat?" he asked. "Or actually a much older one?"

"You're very observant. It's Gladstone's."

"Why are you wearing his hat?"

"I'd like to talk to you about that," I said.

"So you're ready to be that bad man and take me in?" he asked. "I mean, I have that Messiah Movement placard on my lawn. Isn't that enough for the NSA these days?"

"I wouldn't know about that, sir. It seems neither the NSA nor the FBI need my services any longer. I'm not here in any official capacity."

Leonards tried to see me differently and failed. "Are you sure?"

"Want me to show you the badge I don't have as evidence?" I asked, and he laughed.

"You can take the boy out of the bureau, I guess . . ." he said, and stood back from the doorway as he had before, but this time he stepped to the side and offered his home, which was both beautiful and modest. We stood in his living room, and he looked around, hesitating before offering me a seat.

"Y'know what?" he said. "Let's go out to the yard." He gestured through a sliding glass door to an expansive wooden deck that had a palm tree growing right through the middle of it. A bench had been built around the tree, creating a lovely place to sit, but part of me felt I still wasn't something the professor wanted in his home.

He must have come in from the deck to answer the door because there was an old TV still playing, and he went to shut it off before I asked him not to. It was a story about Hamilton Burke.

"Oh, you didn't hear the news?" he asked.

"No."

"He's running for president. They're replaying his announcement."

I watched the crackle and fuzz from Leonards's old TV with its seemingly tech-boosted antennae fully extended and pointed at some local news station. Burke was at Federal Hall in downtown New York, beside Washington's statue, where the very first oath of office was taken—just two blocks from his namesake Alexander Hamilton's grave at Trinity Church, and across the street from the shrapnel that can still be seen in the granite of JP Morgan. Burke was right in the heart of where Gladstone claimed to have met him a year earlier.

"America," he said, "has been very good to me. When I was a young man, America made a promise of great success in exchange for hard work. And let me tell you, I worked very, very hard in the service of that promise. And America did not disappoint. I've received very much for very long, and I deserve everything I've ever earned. I kept my side of the bargain and America kept hers. But those days are over. Today, for far too many hardworking families, America still asks for your labor, your industry, your entrepreneurship, but no longer rewards you with the kind of success I've had. Today, the reward for running full-speed is standing still. Just getting by.

"Now, I'm a businessman. I know you can't get the best out of your people if they're only willing to work hard enough to keep from getting fired. No great company has ever been built on that model, and no nation can remain great with that kind of thinking. We need to restore the promise of America to its people, and that's why today I'm announcing my candidacy for president!"

The crowd erupted into applause, and Burke undid the button on his coal-gray suit, as if the paunch that made his crimson tie curve could receive and repurpose the crowd's energy. "Now, you're going to hear some people say, 'Oh, Hamilton Burke, he's a businessman, what does he know about running this country?' First off, do you know who's going to say that? Politicians. Is that what this country needs more of? I might just be a businessman, but in my world of business you need to show results or get out. So no, I will not be sold short by any man or woman in politician's clothing. And I will never hide from what I am: a man who went into banking, into investments, into real estate, into entertainment, and into technology and figured out how to make things work and how to make money. And that is exactly what America needs now!"

Again, Burke was interrupted by the crowd's enthusiastic ferocity. But there was diversity in the din of approval. There was hope and anger and aggression. All the battling aspirations of the audience were colliding into applause.

"And lastly, let me say that under a Burke White House, not only will this country work, not only will its people work, but the Internet will work!"

Suddenly a different energy erupted. A younger, more fiery passion that rang with glee and longing.

"I condemn the disgraceful, mindless bombing campaigns of Gladstone, the so-called Internet Messiah, but I understand his appeal. The people deserve the Internet. We will get it working—not to appease the terrorist tactics of a madman and his misguided followers but because you, the American people, deserve it."

For the first time, Hamilton lost the crowd. He noticed. While Gladstone's book continued to grow in popularity, and the symbol of his movement had appeared near bombings, the government had not yet made that express association, and no one had taken credit for the attacks.

"So help me, my friends. Help me return the promise of America for all who deserve it. An America where everyone and everything works! Thank you!"

The crowd returned with all their prior enthusiasm, and the old Carly Simon hit from the '80s, "Let the River Run," blasted out of unseen speakers. Burke left in triumph, disappearing into Federal Hall near a banner emblazoned with his name and THE WORKING PARTY as

Carly sang of dreamers waking the nation and the rising silver cities of a new Jerusalem.

"Well, fuck," I said.

"First independent candidate I can see winning," Leonards said. I sat down on his palm-tree-surrounding bench, and he sat opposite me in a folding garden chair. "So. What can I tell you about the Internet?" he asked.

"Actually, that's not why I came here," I said, and Leonards laughed again.

"Of course not!" He took out a little barrel-shaped root-beer hard candy. "Why would anyone want to talk with me about the Internet during an Internet Apocalypse? I only helped invent the thing!"

"Gladstone didn't ask you about the loss either?" I asked, trying to shift the subject back to my target.

"No, he didn't, but that's not my point," he said. "No one in the government has come to talk to me about the loss. Don't you find that odd?"

I considered his point.

"You think I'm being arrogant," he continued. "I mean, sure there are other people to speak with, but not even a consult during a crisis? During Y2K, they flew me to Washington for a briefing."

Seemed the government had no use for either of us, and even though it wasn't my immediate mission statement I decided to explore that. "What would it take for the government to be behind this Apocalypse?"

My stock instantly plummeted in the professor's eyes. I hadn't educated myself about the Internet as I should have, choosing instead to chase and interrogate more knowledgeable men for their alleged misdeeds.

"The government already controls all the hubs," Leonards said with some level of distaste. Fortunately his trust in me seemed to grow as his respect diminished. As a man of science he probably believed stupid people weren't a threat.

"I'm sorry, professor," I said. "This isn't my background. I won't pretend to know what I don't."

"Don't sell yourself short, Agent Rowsdower. That's just about the smartest thing anyone can say."

He offered me a root-beer candy that I declined and then explained the basic plumbing of the Internet. And in many ways it was like plumbing. The Net was just a bunch of global villages tied together at shockingly few points across the world. There was cable under the ocean, literally tying the world together in a very real way rather than some nebulous cloud abstraction. After the Apocalypse happened, the government had taken over the connections, or hubs, in America and restored the Net for a couple of days before going dark again. So yes, my question was naïve. Once the government controlled all those connectors like giant power strips, it was easier to comprehend turning the thing off and on.

"OK," I said. "The government has the means."

"And the opportunity," Leonards continued. "But let's not talk about it like a crime, because it's all perfectly legal. Legal since before the Internet even existed."

"Meaning what?"

"Meaning the Communications Act of 1934 empowers the president to direct communication as he deems essential to national defense," Leonards said. "Right?"

"The gig didn't come with a history primer," I said with too much conviction. "I was a New York fed before being tapped for the NSA, but I saw nothing about the government moving by some legislative decree in the news."

"It's not good copy," Leonards said. "And besides, where would you see it? *Daily Kos* was down with the Net. But I imagine if you went looking, you'd see the administration moved with some conjunction of that law and the Telecommunications Act of '96. That's the one that lets the White House coordinate the activities of its partners in the private sector to eliminate vulnerabilities to cyberattack."

" 'Partners'?" I asked.

"Sure, the Internet has always been partnered between government and the private sector. I told that to Gladstone too, although he didn't seem to care either. It's more than just Gore's bill getting businessmen to lay cable. The private sector even controls, or I should say *controlled*, certain maintenance and security functions."

Years of teaching had served Leonards well. He knew when a student wasn't getting it. "ICANN?" he asked, but rather than triggering an understanding, it was just one more thing I didn't know.

"I appreciate that you're not a computer scientist, Agent Rowsdower," he said. "I also appreciate that you spent the majority of your career looking for bad guys. Murderers, mobsters, drug dealers, what-have-you. But don't you find it curious that when the government gave you a new job, they didn't even give you enough information to ask the right questions?"

"I do, sir," I said, "and at the moment of my learning, I was no longer needed. So yes, professor, I get it. Tell me about ICANN."

"It's technical," he said. "And they have many functions, but to dumb it down, no offense, they're tasked with making the Internet work. They assign and verify Internet addresses, running the protocols to make sure the Net is not vulnerable to cyberattacks."

"What kind of cyberattacks?" I asked.

"Any kind. Could be phishing schemes based on fraudulent email addresses designed to steal credit-card information or, far worse, invalid sites, misdirecting searches and breaking the Net, so to speak. Do you remember the early days of the Apocalypse? It was more like that at times. Stuff just didn't work right, followed by periodic blackouts. ICANN holds the keys to DNSSEC, the security specifications that verify the web's content, keeps it working."

"What do you mean 'keys'?"

"Well, there is the master key, which contains the code to run the security protocols, that's kept in a Fort Knox safe. That's the key that's necessary to reboot the security protocol in case the Internet goes down in cyberattack. And there are three crypto officers spread all over the world that have the actual keys to that safe. There are also recovery-key shareholders who have bits of the master key who can rebuild that key in case the physical plant is destroyed and something happens to the crypto officers."

"Seriously?"

"Seriously."

"You're pretty up on this stuff," I said.

"Don't you follow the news about your children, Mr. Rowsdower?"

"I don't have any kids," I said, and left it at that. There was no reason to talk about Madeline. Not just because it wasn't his business or that it wouldn't help me, but because I no longer even felt like that man. The man who thought he'd be a father. Who wondered how he was going to balance his career drive with family before every-thing was made far simpler by leukemia.

But even under Gladstone's hat, Leonards saw things I didn't want to show. "I'm very sorry," he said, and must have meant it too because he didn't object when I pulled out an American Spirit cigarette. I offered him one.

"You won't get rid of me that easily, Agent Rows-dower," he replied.

"Please, call me Aaron," I said. "And I'm not trying to get rid of you at all. I'm trying to find Gladstone."

"I'm sorry, Aaron," he said, "but I'm not sure I can help you with that. I only met Gladstone once, and the only thing I really know about him is he barely knew more about the Net than you. So is now the time you tell me why you're wearing his hat?"

I told the professor all I had to tell, and as bluntly as I could. Not just because I knew he'd appreciate the effi-ciency of clean logic but because the job had taught me that one of the perks of speaking to highly successful people is that insecurities don't get in the way. They don't need compliments and they don't mind disagreement. It is very hard to slight a truly great man, because the world has already confirmed his worth, and nothing removes petty insecurity like global anointment.

"So you believe in a conspiracy," he asked, "that con-nects the forces who stole the Internet, those who cost you your job, and those who framed Gladstone?"

"I do."

"And these bombings. Who's behind that?"

"I'm not sure. Possibly the same people, in an attempt to vilify Gladstone. Or maybe actual terrorists or anarchists seizing upon instability. Perhaps misguided members of the Internet Reclamation Movement."

"'Misguided,'" he said. "Does that mean you think Gladstone might still be involved to some degree?"

"No, quite frankly, aside from it not being in the nature of the man I met, I just don't think he's capable of organizing something like that."

Leonards laughed. "Well, then, if Gladstone's that useless, why are you so bent on finding him?"

"Not because of what he can do but because of what he knows."

"You think it's one bogeyman after him? One bad man acting alone?"

"No. I imagine it takes many bad, or at least compromised, people to keep the world offline, but, y'know," I said, smiling as I dropped an ash between the floorboards of Leonards's deck, "sometimes one bad man can make a difference."

"And what will you do if you find Gladstone? What he cannot?"

"I hadn't gotten that far yet. I just want to know what we're up against. Surely you can tell me something about him."

"Y'know, I've gotten a little peculiar in my old age," Leonards said. I waited. I could tell he was about to go professorial. "Remember that story in the days before the Net went down about that hitchhiking robot?"

I remembered something I hadn't bothered to read about a robot getting its electronic brains beaten out, but I wasn't sure we were talking about the same thing.

"Is that the robot that got destroyed in Philly?" I asked.

"The very same," he said. "I built it to see if it was possible for something relying on the kindness of strangers to make it around the world."

"Why?"

"Because I'm an eighty-year-old computer genius. What do you want me to do? Watch *Matlock* reruns until I die?"

"Sorry."

"Anyway, I wanted to see how far it could go and how much it could learn about humanity. Absolute strangers saw this hitchhiking robot with just a few instructions on its back and cared for him. Traveled with him and left him for others to do the same. It made it all through Germany. Germany! And then the Netherlands. It survived New York and Boston until a bunch of hooligans tore it to pieces in Philadelphia."

"The City of Brotherly Love," I scoffed.

"Believe me," he said, "the irony wasn't lost on me, but that's not the point. The point was this robot, which had a rudimentary personality chip, was also learning. Learning about the world, and like any child he learned from what he saw, and applied it to everything he did and everyone he met thereafter. And the sad part is, because people were so kind to him at the start of his life, so good to him, he never saw the evil coming. He had no way of dealing with it. No defenses."

Leonard cleared his throat, because even though he was touched, he was not the kind of man to let sentimentality get in the way of discourse, at least not when talking about evil in the world. "Anyway," he said. "I built the hitchhiking robot to learn something, and if I built him again, do you know what I'd do differently?"

"Keep him the fuck out of Philadelphia?"

"I'm being serious. What do you think I'd change?"

"I don't know."

"Absolutely nothing."

"You wouldn't build up his defenses? His distrust?" I asked.

"No. Because if you start closed like that, you never open up fully. You never get where you're going."

"I don't think I understand," I said, and he sized me up one final time.

"You ever think about Exodus?" he asked.

"The Bible? I'm not the most religious guy."

"Well, in the Exodus from Egypt, Moses raised his staff, so the story goes, and with the power of God, split the Red Sea, allowing the Hebrews to escape to freedom."

"Right," I said. "I saw the movie."

"I'm sure, but the thing is, you ever think about the Jew at the very back of the line?"

"What do you mean?"

"I mean to him, something of that magnitude over this crowd of people before him must have looked terrifying."

"OK . . ."

"And yet, to be free, he had to keep walking. He had to see a power great enough to split an ocean in two, and walk right into it."

I didn't speak, and the professor moved his folding chair closer to where I was sitting, looking more certain than I'd yet seen from this very certain man. "Miracles and disasters look the same in the distance," he said. "But the trick is not running for cover. Greatness requires the ability to be destroyed by the world and the faith to believe you won't be."

I let go of a slow breath and looked at the cracks in the floorboards. I'd received a significant gift that made nothing clearer. "Thank you, Professor, but I'd hoped you'd tell me something about Gladstone. . . ."

He was disappointed. "If I hear from Gladstone," he said, "I'll be sure to tell him you have his hat."

I couldn't be mad at Leonards. He was a wealth of knowledge, even if it wasn't what I needed at the moment. Still, my years on the job had taught me nothing is wasted. And not all was lost, because Leonards was the last thing keeping me in L.A. Being out of both work and leads meant I could go back home again. My real home. New York.

The next day, I was on a plane flying east and wondering if I was traveling farther from or closer to Gladstone. I didn't know where to find him, and I was still convinced nothing more could happen before I did. And even though no threat had been directed at me, I felt I wouldn't truly be safe until I knew what he knew. I got my bags at JFK and splurged on a livery cab driver to take me home to Queens.

The place was just as I left it, and no one asked me where I'd been. No one in the White Castle on Northern Boulevard. No one on Bell Boulevard as I tugged my suitcase with one hand and ate a slider with another. Queens didn't need me to exist, just like the world

went on without the Internet. I was home and somehow felt more alone than I did in L.A. I got to my apartment building. Paper memes were now in some of the
windows. Gladstone's hat-wearing Wi-Fi symbol with
different messages written underneath. I couldn't read
what they said, but that wasn't the point. Gladstone had
left more of a mark on my building than I had, and just
when I reached a point where I was starting to think I
didn't exist, Margo saved me.

She was waiting for me in the apartment doorway, standing five-foot-ten in a red sundress, and looking
sensational.

"Well, Aaron Rowsdower! As I live and breathe," she
said in some corny Southern accent, but it didn't matter
what she said. She was standing there, seeing me, and I
wanted to take her in my arms. I felt like a boy filled with
new feelings he didn't understand, I wanted to tell her
all of that. Instead, I stopped and said, "What the fuck?"

"I just got here, like, ten seconds ago." She smiled.

"How is that possible? I didn't even tell you I was going
back to New York."

"Well, I certainly knew you weren't going to stay
in L.A. Besides, Information only had a New York address for you."

"You came all the way to New York on the chance I'd
be here?"

"Don't be so flattered. It's not like you live in Des
Moines. If you weren't home, I'm sure I could find stuff
to do."

I wheeled my suitcase up to her. "Well, I have to put
my stuff down. Do you want to come up, or grab a
bite . . . ?"

"Leave it packed," she said. "We're going to London."

"What?"

She reached into a tiny black-and-white handbag and pulled out a letter. It had no envelope. "It's for you," she said.

I leaned in to take the letter. We were close enough to touch.

Dear Special Agent Rowsdower,

I need your help, but I'm not ready to be found. At least you'll be happy to know I'm not in Los Angeles. Go to England. 38 Lancaster Road, East London.

Cautiously optimistic,

Gladstone

Part II

Report 4

I had a lot of questions, but a six-hour transatlantic flight provides plenty of Q&A opportunities. Margo had insisted on two things: coming along and buying the tickets. It wasn't in my nature to accept either of those requirements. While I no longer had a badge, I didn't need to be teaming with a civilian, and while I still had my pension (graciously offered to me with my termination despite being two years shy of full qualification), I didn't want to feel like a charity case, having people pay my way.

"Don't be stupid," she said. "This is tax-deductible for me. I'm following up on the Gladstone story. What I optioned doesn't have an ending."

I was reticent. "I don't know what we're walking into, and I don't even have a gun."

"Don't worry," she said. "It's England. No one else will either."

Margo seemed to have forgiven me for interrogating

her too aggressively at the hospital. Our relationship was on the mend like the scar below her collarbone.

"Can I see the envelope for that letter from Gladstone?" I asked.

"I didn't bring it, but it *was* a UK postmark."

"How's your miner doing?" I asked.

"What's that got to do with the Internet?" she asked.

"Not a thing."

We stopped speaking for a bit until she pulled a manila folder from her purse. It had magazine clippings in it, and when she handed it over in a neat but very tactile pile of index cards, paper clips, notes, and glossy articles, it was very easy to imagine her as a talented junior high student in the nondigital age.

I read through the articles. She'd looked up the address we were going to, and it wasn't some flophouse for a visiting American. It was the offices of Tech Global—a technology company I didn't fully understand, and helmed by a Neville Bhattacharyya.

I pulled out the last article. "He's one of the ICANN key holders?"

"Crypto officers, yeah. You know about that?" Margo asked.

"Just what Professor Leonards told me. Something about three people with the keys to reboot the Internet?"

"Well, not exactly," Margo said. "Keys to reboot the security protocols to verify the addresses of the Net in case of cyberattack."

"Right," I said. "But I gotta say, for a wannabe film producer, you really just stepped all over the drama there."

"Fair point. I'll try to work some Horcruxes into the

script, but for now, I was more interested in correctly understanding the background of whom we're meeting."

I must have made a face because Margo asked what was wrong. "Nothing," I said. "I've just never flown with someone who used 'whom' in casual conversation."

"Well, I'm a classy dame," she said, and I tried not to think about how much I liked her. Not for the rest of the flight, and not later in the hotel as I tried to sleep without hearing her every move on the other side of the wall.

The next day, we sat in the Starbucks of a London office building and tried to plan the attack. I wasn't used to the disadvantages of being a civilian. No badge to flash. No threats to make. I wasn't even in my own country.

Worse, there was only the vaguest focus for our discussion if we got to Neville. Still, the less I knew, the more marching orders I gave: find Neville, then find Gladstone, then find our common enemy, and understand who was behind the Apocalypse. I write these words like they were some internal monologue, but they weren't. I spilled them out over coffee and Margo listened, occasionally challenging me just enough to make me understand things more clearly.

"Why do you say anyone's after you?" she asked.

"What do you mean? Wasn't I just let go after twenty years on the job?"

"Well, yes," she said. "But you released Gladstone. Twice. And then he killed his ex-wife and committed an act of terrorism. Someone had to pay for that."

"Wait, now you think Gladstone's a murdering terrorist?"

"No, of course not. I agree he was set up and someone's definitely after him. They killed his ex-wife, framed him, and are committing acts of terrorism in his name. Now *that's* a conspiracy, but you . . . well, you might have been collateral damage."

It was a valid point, and I didn't know what to say so I kept drinking my black coffee. Thankfully the correcting forces of corporate franchise had prevented the Brits from fucking up my coffee by doing anything too culturally weird.

"So you're saying the conspiracy might be more fractured than I've thought? That Gladstone got fucked by evil and I got fucked by the bureaucracy's reaction to evil?"

Margo put her coffee down after a slow, happy sip. "Well, well, Special Agent Rowsdower," she said. "You might have a bit of a poet in you after all."

"I'd rather have an in with Neville," I said.

"I have the in," she said, and pulled a nicely bound copy of Gladstone's journal, *Notes from the Internet Apocalypse*, out of her bag and put it on the table between us. "Did you notice, Aaron, that we are *not* the only people here with this book?"

I looked around. Incredibly, it was true. Gladstone's stupid panic attack of a journal, chronicling his drunken "investigation" throughout New York, had spread to the UK. And in this Internetless world, it seemingly had taken the place of many of the laptops typically visible in coffee shops.

"Jesus Christ," I said. "Everyone is reading that thing. Not doing wonders for my reputation."

"Don't worry. We'll get a good-looking guy to play you in the movie."

"So what's your angle?" I asked.

"We go in smooth," Margo said. "No investigation. No crime. I drop my Prague Rock Productions card and say we're looking for movie consultants. He'll talk. Everyone likes movies."

Two hours later we were both in Neville Bhattacharyya's office. Margo was that good. Recognizing him by his picture and seeing him enter the building around nine forty-five, she cut for the elevator bank near the security desk and forced a collision so effortlessly you would have thought she was raised by pickpockets on the streets of some Third World nation. But that wasn't what sold it. Instead, she dropped to her knees right in front of him, gathering the possessions she'd deliberately let fall, then met his eyes from below before slowly rising to her full five-foot-ten. I saw them exchange words from the Starbucks as he coughed and made an extra effort to maintain eye contact instead of letting his stare linger on the modest V-cut of Margo's blouse. He gestured to Gladstone's journal prominently displayed in her gathered possessions, and she gave Neville her card, sealing the deal.

"You didn't find that a bit degrading?" I asked when she came to get me.

"To an extent," she said, "but far less degrading than sitting in a Starbucks and failing."

Margo told Neville I was a technical consultant on her film as well, and we sat in his office while she did most of the talking. It was a far messier workspace than I'd imagined for a tech person, and pictures of his kids permeated the strange mix of opulent Old English leather and mahogany that clashed with the minimalist steel-and-glass bookshelves overflowing with electronics. I also counted no fewer than three ashtrays. I was surprised to see smoking allowed in a twenty-first-century office, but after lighting up, he flicked a switch on some sort of powerful vacuum/filtration system living in his drop ceiling. The smoke visibly lifted up and away.

"It's good to be the boss," he said before spoiling his moment with a hacking cough. No filtration system would keep away what was coming for him.

Margo started asking about ICANN, and he started a rote speech about the honor that had been bestowed upon him by the technological community. I zoned out for a bit, but while he explained that ICANN was an independent, private, international body tasked by the US Department of Commerce, I noticed something in Neville's office besides papers and cigarettes: a picture of him and Hamilton Burke. The two men happy in their tuxedos. Neville was heavier and happier than he appeared now.

"I see you know our future president," I said, and pointed to the photo, which looked to have been taken a good five years earlier, Neville's skin a richer hue than today's ashen color.

"Oh, this?" he said, taking the picture off the bookcase behind him. "Yeah, I met Hamilton Burke a couple of years ago. Some fund-raiser. He was a Republican then. None of this 'Working Party' stuff."

"You and Hamilton still go bowling much?" I asked, hiding my surprise at how relatively recent the photo was.

He put the picture back and reclaimed his cigarette from the ashtray. "For folks looking for information on the Internet, you certainly seem motivated to find facts on people."

"The Internet is people," Margo said.

"And we're still here," I added.

I leaned back in my chair and pulled out the first of my three allotted cigarettes for the day. "Will that filter of yours work for non-bosses too?" I asked, and held my lighter in half tilt waiting for permission.

"Feel free," he said, and Margo jumped in to rekindle the tech-speak of moments earlier.

"Mr. Bhattacharyya, as an outside observer I was hoping you could help me understand something about the Net that I can't seem to get a handle on. Net Neutrality?"

"What it is?" he asked, trying to gauge the level of Margo's ignorance, or purported ignorance.

"Well, I get the concept. We don't want the private sector to run wild. I mean, if certain sites like Fox News could bribe cable providers to have their site load faster while something like MSNBC loaded with the speed of dial-up, that would be a bad thing."

"Would it?" Neville asked. "I'd like to see them both meet a nasty demise, frankly, but I take your meaning. The Internet, as you say, is people. But it's also information. It runs on an incredibly expensive infrastructure, and in that way it's also like a public utility."

"And if the government were to take it over?" I asked.

"Yes, what if that?" he asked. "Every government has its interests. They could monetize it differently. Governments like to do that. Tolls on roads. Fees. Maybe the Internet would be like your phone with data-usage amounts. That money could build a lot of bombs. Or maybe your fears about evil Fox News could be just as likely under a government-controlled Net. Maybe sites critical of the administration wouldn't load as fast, or lose their verifications, or whatever."

"But that's not what Net Neutrality is, is it? Governmental control in place of the private sector?"

"You're correct. That's just what the conservatives in your country fear it is, but honestly, there are two reasons all bets are off regarding this issue. First, what I said was my explanation in a non-Apocalypse setting. Who knows what the conditions of a restored Net will be. But more important, and forgive me for saying so as a non-citizen of your fair country, but with massive consolidation and super PACs, the private sector has more influence over your government than ever before. Hell, you even have a billionaire running for president. So when it comes to who's controlling a non-neutral Net, government or business, well, that might get increasingly hard to tell."

He reached for another cigarette and noticed mine was still burning.

"American Spirits," I said. "No additives to make them burn faster. See? America's good for something." I offered him the pack and he took one.

"Wait a tic," he said. "Aaron Rowsdower? Special Agent Rowsdower from Gladstone's book?"

"That's me," I said, and he got confused.

"Hmm," he said and took a long drag of his cigarette. "Your teeth look perfectly normal to me."

I laughed. "Thank you, sir. Well, Gladstone wasn't really in the best place when he wrote that."

"Yes, tell me about this Gladstone fellow," he said.

"You don't know him?" I asked.

"Why would I know him?"

I was going to say *Because he told us to come here*, but that was wrong. There was no need to show that card, and Margo knew it too, because she jumped right in and asked, "What would you like to know?"

"Anything you like. Is he a messiah? Is he a terrorist?"

"Are those the only choices?" Margo asked.

"Well, with all this commotion," Neville said, "he's got to be *something*," and I remembered what Professor Leonards said about disasters and miracles looking the same in the distance.

"I can tell you something about Gladstone," Margo said, sitting forward in her chair. "He believes in pure things."

She had Neville's attention, and having gotten it, she proceeded to tell a story about a college-aged Gladstone who witnessed a poor father take his three small girls to a dollar store and proudly announce they could get anything they wanted. Apparently, the girls squealed in delight and scurried inside like royalty. Margo was repeating what Gladstone must have told her, but it was no merely echoed narrative. She was feeling what he must have felt. She was struck that this father, who had nothing, managed to create a happy moment for his children through the sheer force of will. But it was more than that, she said. It was knowing the possibility existed, even in this world, that by the time these girls realized how desperately poor they'd grown up, it would be too late because they would've already had a happy childhood.

Neville tapped the American Spirit into his ashtray while looking at a framed picture of his kids by its side. "Well, that's a lovely story, but sometimes, 'possibility' isn't quite enough when your children's futures are involved."

We'd crossed a mark, and I knew the window was closing. "Before we leave you, Mr. Neville," I said, "do you have a theory on who's behind this Apocalypse?"

"Well, if I knew that, *I'd* be the Internet Messiah." We waited for more instead of laughing, and he continued, "I'm sorry. I can't help you."

"That's all right," Margo said. "You've been wonderful, but that's another thing I could tell you about Gladstone. He believes we're all the Messiah. Anyone who believes. Anyone in the fight."

"That's another lovely story, isn't it?" he said.

"Yes," Margo replied, and stood to say goodbye.

Neville stood too, and Margo extended her hand quickly. A friendly handshake that kept the desk between them. "Thank you *so* much," she said, and gave him another of her cards. "I hope we can call on you again?"

"Of course. It was a pleasure."

I dropped the rest of my cigarettes on his desk. Now even three a day seemed too much. "A gift from your friends in the States," I said, and touched the brim of Gladstone's hat in a polite salute.

I wanted to grab lunch and compare notes, but Margo said she was eager to get back to the hotel. She'd worn heels to make an impression and was apparently dying for some flats. We hailed a cab just as a bank of clouds covered the sun.

"Whaddya think of our friend upstairs," I asked, and she replied, "You mean God?" but her heart wasn't in it. She was too preoccupied.

"What's wrong?"

"There's something I haven't told you," she said, and it suddenly got even darker outside.

"Looks like we're in for it," I said, trying to detect any trace of the sunny day that had just vanished.

"Oh, this is nothing," Margo said. "You've never been to England before?"

"No, ma'am, but let me guess, you backpacked here as a college kid."

"Something like that. The Royal Albert Hall is coming up."

I looked through the darkness and traffic to see if I could catch a glimpse, but just at that moment, we heard a sound like a truck colliding with something frail. A boom followed by tumbling pieces, but it wasn't thunder or rain. The traffic stopped, and those English sirens I knew only from TV and movies started going off. This was more than a traffic accident, but I still had a stupid Beatles joke rattling around my head about someone who "blew his mind out in a car." Thankfully, I kept my mouth shut because soon I saw smoke in the distance. And as we crept closer we could see the damage.

Later, the police would tell us about the pipe bombs, about the handful of people killed and the dozen more injured, but in the moment all we could see was the majestic hall and what was missing. There was evidence of several explosions. Synchronized destruction leaving smoke and darkness in sections where ornate brickwork and windows were supposed to be. And in those spaces, black smoke poured out, sometimes penetrated by darting flames that brought only more destruction without adding light.

"How many holes does it take to fill the Albert Hall?" I heard Margo ask.

"That's not funny," I replied, but she didn't need to be told. She was crying, fumbling for the locks, until she was free of the cab and running. I threw some money at the cabbie without bothering to count denominations and chased after her.

"What are you doing?" I called, but she just kept running towards the destruction. I caught up to her and grabbed her wrist.

"Let go of me!" she screamed, and she was mad, almost violent, but I didn't let go. I just held her differently—firm, but not forceful—and made sure she could see me when I asked, "Where are you going, Margo?"

"To help," she said.

"You can't help. Look, the ambulances are on their way. What can you do?"

"I don't know. Something! Give blood."

"OK, I understand," I said. "Let's give blood. We'll give blood."

She let me lead her, gently, back to the cab, still crying all the tears she'd managed to hold back at the Formosa Cafe. At the hospital, they had us side by side on cots as we and many others held out our arms for the victims. We bled and watched the news about those who didn't bleed by choice. The dead were dead, and the injured were injured. Only a tiny fraction of people would need our blood. There was no shortage. Margo's blood, my blood, and the blood of every Brit in a line that ran out the door would be largely useless to the survivors of this tragedy, but that wasn't the point. We all knew that before we ever went to the hospital. The point was bleeding. To suffer a prick, to feel a loss, to bleed. Because not bleeding when surrounded by tragedy feels shameful. So we gave and as they pulled the needle from Margo's arm, I saw her fight every impulse to grab it back and give more. She had more to give. She wanted to give until it hurt so much that she couldn't tell it apart from the hurt that was already there.

"What did you want to tell me?" I asked in the cab back to the hotel. "Y'know, before the bombing."

"I wasn't completely honest with you," she said, and my stomach tightened up.

"I got more than one letter from Gladstone."

I waited, scared of getting a confession I didn't want. To be told this was all Gladstone. That he planned this bombing. That she knew everything and was complicit.

She continued. "There were *two* letters in the envelope to me. One I gave you in Queens, and another one that Gladstone asked me to give you now."

"Whaddya mean, Gladstone asked you?"

"Good point," Margo said. "There were three letters. The one I gave you in Queens, this one, and a third one telling me when to give you each letter, but that was really more of a Post-it."

She pulled out a sealed envelope addressed to me, "Special Agent Rowsdower," and I wondered if the title were a sign of respect or Gladstone mocking me at the loss of my job.

I pulled out the letter. It was not a confession. It was another task. A request for help.

Dear Special Agent Rowsdower,
Thank you for coming to London. Thank you for doing what I cannot do while I'm in hiding for things I haven't done and would never do.

Regarding that, there are two more men who also didn't commit the crimes they're accused of, and are sitting indefinitely in your old stomping grounds of the L.A. Veterans' Affairs Building.

I think you know Jeeves and Tobey are innocent, and if you have any doubt, I can help you. The entire area surrounding the Hollywood sign was under video surveillance. In the moment, I thought that surveillance would be down because of the Apocalypse, but that was stupid, because the surveillance was a closed system. If footage still exists, it might show the helicopter that destroyed the Hollywood sign. Terror from above as the three of us ran screaming.

You will need the help of Anonymous, which is scary. You know where to find them. You might remember Quiffmonster42 from my book, I don't know if you'll find him there, but he is not to be trusted. He is not our friend.

Cautiously optimistic,
Gladstone

P.S. "Special Agent" is meant to be a sign of respect.

"We're going back to New York?" I asked.

"Is that what it says?" she replied, and I handed her the letter.

"Why did he send us to London, just to go back to New York?"

Margo finished reading the letter and smiled. "Because he wanted to make sure he could trust you before he asked you to help his friends."

"And why are you smiling?"

"Because he likes you, Aaron."

Report 5

If Gladstone were here, he might write something like, "When the Net came back, it was nothing like we expected," but he's not, so I'll tell things my way. The Net came back, but not the Net we lost. Not the one we were looking for.

The day after Margo and I got back from London, the president gave an address from the Oval Office to tell America the news: the Apocalypse was over. He didn't say "Apocalypse," because using that word to describe technical difficulties in the face of actual exploding buildings and death would have made him look like a prick. Instead, he said he was pleased to report that after much hard work, the Internet would be restored. The government had taken over the hubs long ago and kept them secure. He explained this would be an ongoing process that could not be left solely to the private sector without fear of another attack. The world, he said, was connected by cable, in a very real way, and physical or cyberattacks at a handful of key connection points around the world could keep millions in the dark. In addition to the hub occupation, the navy was now "supervising and supplementing" the private sector by patrolling the miles of cable beneath the ocean floor, keeping us working.

Then he referenced the bombings at the Farmers Market, the San Francisco movie theater, and outside the Formosa Cafe, and how even though the Wi-Fi symbol had accompanied each of the bombings, no one had claimed official responsibility for any of the attacks save for Penn Station and Disney World. The president did not directly reference the Royal Albert Hall bombing, and not just because it was overseas but because a terrorist group seeking, not the Internet, but the removal of any Western presence in the Middle East had taken credit for that one. They'd also promised more attacks throughout the West, and to the extent that the United States must always remain vigilant against terrorism in all its forms, Obama pledged the government's dedication to the preservation of the Net.

Then he paused before explaining further that not all threats to "our Internet and our security" were as simple as maintaining connections. The "connectivity problem," as he called it, had been fixed fairly quickly, but the best and brightest in our government had spent the last several months undoing cyberattacks and rebooting the safety protocols that verified each and every web address and email. That work was vital because each website, he explained, whether it was Amazon or your bank, had a discrete address made up of numbers. In a secure Internet, you could just type in the name of the site and get there without remembering those codes, because an organization called ICANN verified that address. That meant that when you typed in "Bank of America" and deposited $1,000, your money really went to you and not the private bank account of some scammer who'd hijacked the Net.

In closing, it was explained that all these additional security protocols required millions of additional hours of labor and expense, but that it was worth it to return the Internet, a source of "communication and illumination" to the people. However, to cover this ongoing expense, to keep the Internet safe and working, it would need to be monetized differently going forward. Internet use would be a little more like the data plans associated with smart phones, in the sense that you'd pay more if you used more. In addition to the fees already in place to the private sector, your cable providers, and paid sites, there would now be a usage fee paid to the government. Much like other public utilities like water and electricity, this was just a monthly expense to keep the Net flowing into our homes.

There was little protest in the days that followed. That's how people are. They want normalcy and they'll pay for it. Even the television that Margo and I were watching came with a post-Apocalypse cost. In the months that followed the crash, my building had collected $500 from all the tenants to install a powerful antenna which picked up the old-fashioned broadcasts that the networks were now amping up, and fed them to the tenants. No one was sure if that was a fair price for this technological workaround, but no one questioned it too much. It was just nice to have reception. So now this was just one more cost. One more way to be nickeled and dimed, but hopefully for something everyone wanted.

I turned to Margo to see her take on the feasibility of this new Internet. She was in dark blue blouse and skirt, but seemed as comfortable as someone wearing sweat-pants and a T-shirt as she sat with her feet under her, drinking a vodka soda.

"Whaddya think?" I asked.

"I think," she said, downing her drink and reaching for her shoes, "that if Obama's bringing back the Net, then we better get to that 4chan/Anonymous meetup, while they're still having them."

She was right. I'd read Gladstone's book and interro-gated enough suspects to know that the loose collective of hackers, anarchists, and activists known as Anony-mous shared a certain overlap with the depraved, meme-generating site formerly known as 4chan, and I also knew they'd been meeting every Tuesday night during the Apocalypse. When the Net came back, I assumed they'd go back underground into their digital holes.

"Fuck, you're right. Time to hit the Bowery."

"Lucky that today's Tuesday," she said.

"Well, it *was* a one-in-seven chance. . . ."

"Were you just quoting Gladstone's book?" she asked.

"Was I?"

"Maybe. Doesn't matter. Y'know, you two are more alike than you know."

I didn't say anything. It took all my energy to under-stand she meant it as a compliment.

———

We walked the block from Penn Station to the B/D downtown on Sixth, but they didn't come. Instead, we were greeted by a train far too wide and green. There was a laminate stuck to one of the car windows reading NEW YORK MUSEUM OF TRANSPORTATION. It seemed some sort of recommissioned R-6 train was running on the BDFM tracks, and just in case the car didn't send enough of a message, there were already passengers aboard, either actors or happy participants, dressed in period clothes.

Margo and I stepped inside the car and saw the museum had also hired a four-piece to play swing jazz right there in the center of our military gray/green car. Bare lightbulbs hung every two or three feet and ceiling fans spun. I wanted to ask one of the period-dressed passengers if this novelty train was still making the normal stops, but there was too much risk that one of the drama-school extras would commit to character, saying something like, "The B train? Whatever do you mean? I'm not familiar with that subway line—what with this being 1946 and all!" I tried to look out the window for evidence of scheduled stops, but Margo grabbed my hand and pulled me a few steps to a less crowded space. Then she started doing what could only be called her best impersonation of a flapper-influenced freestyle jazz dance. Some tourists took pictures with their iPads, not just because of the attractive lady shaking it in the aisles, but because with Gladstone's fedora and my sports jacket, they must have assumed I was part of the show.

"Holy shit, that was fun," Margo said after we reached the Bowery.

"I'm glad something about this night will be. I'm not

looking forward to spending time with these . . . what are they called again? /b/tards?"

"Yep, after the /b/ boards on 4chan, where Anonymous originated."

"Right. And what were the /b/boards again?"

"Basically just a place to post filthy images, hatred, memes. Y'know, stupid shit."

"I can't tell you how happy I am Gladstone has us looking for brilliant tech collaborators in a den of meme-loving imbeciles."

"Eh, geniuses, fools," Margo said. "Everyone loves a good fart joke."

Outside the Bowery Poetry Club, there was an attendant wearing a bag over his head with the eyes and mouth cut out, just like in Gladstone's journal. And also like in the journal, the guy was a prick.

"Password?" he asked.

"I'm Special Agent Aaron N. Rowsdower of the NET Recovery Act," I said, hoping to bluff my way in.

Even through the bag holes, I could see his surprise. "The dude from Gladstone's book?" he asked.

"Yes."

He paused. "What?" I asked.

"I dunno. Your teeth look normal to me," he said, and Margo laughed.

"Oh tits," he proclaimed, noticing Margo for the first time. "Come in!"

Inside, things were a little less predictable. Gladstone had written about juvenile meetups filled with boyish joy-buzzer pranks. A gathering brimming with desperate attempts to re-create real-life mischief in place of what they'd lost online. A waitress had brought him novelty ice cubes with bugs inside, and one of the clan stole his jacket and hat, but we were not greeted by an explosion of bad behavior and noise. Instead, most sat quietly at their white-linen tables for four, each with a tiny white candle. And even though they were masked, there was a familiarity in the crowd. They were anonymous, in name and identity, but they were the same anonymous to one another week after week, and that proximity had bred some manners that Groucho glasses and half masks couldn't quite destroy.

A replay of Obama's speech was playing on a loop as Margo and I found a table. I hung my tweed sports jacket on the back of my chair and placed Gladstone's hat on the table. By the time my Johnnie Walker and Margo's vodka soda arrived, a man in a red velvet robe and Guy Fawkes mask (one of the few masks so ceremonial in the audience) appeared onstage.

"Think that's Quiffmonster42?" I asked Margo.

"I don't know," she whispered. "He's wearing a *mask*."

"Greetings, Anonymous," he said in a voice that was far too nasal for the solemnity of this presentation. "The president says the Internet is returning to us. What do we make of this?"

There was applause. A few woots. Enough general approval to show appreciation, but tempered with a distrust that came second-nature to this group.

"I've watched this speech many times," the man said, "and it occurs to me, Obama never says who actually took the Internet, who disabled it, just that we need the government to bring it back. For a fee. And I'd like you to consider what that means while we scroll through this week's board submissions."

And as is the way of 4chan, talk turned quickly from conspiracy to cocks. A slide show started on the screen behind Fawkes's head. First, there was a picture of Obama from the recent speech with a penis Photoshopped into one of his raised hands and a vagina in the other, and the phrase CONNECTIVITY PROBLEMS? in thick, drop-shadow Impact font below. That got a minimal response, and Fawkes clicked to the next one. A picture of the newly announced Republican presidential candidate, Sen. Melissa Bramson with an ejaculating penis Photoshopped next to her face. That got slightly more of a reaction, particularly from one guy to our right, who was snorting through the nose holes of his mask. When I looked closer, I saw his disguise was a cheap plastic fedora, covered in felt with a nondescript attached face plate that hung down, covering only the eyes and nose.

"What kind of mask is that?" I asked Margo.

She got really excited. "Oh, good!" she said.

"What?"

"It's a Gladstone mask," she said. "I had them commissioned after I bought the rights. Did a first soft launch in New York two weeks ago, but this is the first one I've seen out in the world."

"Why'd you do that?"

"Whaddya mean, why? I'm building buzz, getting a mark established. I've also printed up thousands of those blank Gladstone memes with the Wi-Fi symbol for people to put in their windows and cars."

"Really?"

"Yes, I told you I used to be in 'branding.' I'm protecting my investment. Just makes sense."

I widened my eyes and smirked.

"What's so funny?" she asked.

"Apparently, the revolution will be monetized."

Just then the crowd groaned because Fawkes had flipped to the next slide, which was an extreme close-up of a medical textbook picture of an untreated syphilitic penis. Margo turned from the screen and looked at me in wonder. "Do you know Gladstone made that exact same revolution pun when I told him my plan?"

I got angrier than I expected. "Hey, if you'd like, maybe I could borrow that dude's Gladstone mask and you can just pretend he's sitting right here with you?"

That's when the Hamilton Burke pic went up, and wouldn't you know it, there was a cock Photoshopped into his hand, a lot like the others, along with the phrase below, reading "WORKING IT" PARTY. That got the fewest laughs, and Fawkes stopped the display.

"Jesus, guys," he said. "Is that all we've got this week? Shit's getting old."

Clearly the fifty to a hundred and fifty regulars at the Bowery Poetry Club were no match for the old content creation that drew upon the cock-based talents of millions from all over the world. It was an interesting consideration. An infinite number of monkeys at typewriters could eventually come up with *Hamlet*, but a hundred guys in the tri-state area were mostly limited to dicks. In any event, I'd seen enough penises for one night.

"Attention, /b/tards!" I said. "I'm Special Agent Rowsdower, and I have some questions for you."

A silence fell over the crowd, and I was impressed with the amount of respect I could command with even a false title, but just at that moment, one of the collective charged from my right, and grabbed my jacket and hat.

"Look at me," he said, placing the hat on his head. "Identity theft! I'm Special Agent Rowsdower!" Or at least that's what he would have said, if I'd let him finish his sentence instead of punching him right in the teeth, the moment he got to "Special." He fell straight down and I reclaimed my hat from his head before he even hit the floor. Another man, wearing a Gladstone mask no less, charged me from the left and probably would have gotten the jump on me, except that Margo subtly extended her elegant and very long right leg, tripping up my would-be assailant and sending him headfirst into the adjacent table.

"Gentlemen!" Fawkes shouted. "Enough!"

That upset the guy I'd punched in the teeth, who started to protest. "But he punched—"

"But nothing, Sergeant Turd. You had it coming. You've been doing that same identity-theft joke to every noob who's stepped in here for over a year. Now, please. Let's allow our guest to make his statement. What was that name again, sir?"

"Special Agent Rowsdower."

"Why don't you try again?"

"Why?"

"Well, because there *was* a Special Agent Rowsdower. And in fact, he's fairly well known round these parts, what with Gladstone's journal and all. But the thing is, *that* Special Agent Rowsdower went off to work in L.A., where he was relieved of his duties several months ago. So, if you please sir, your name again?"

"How do you know that?"

"We know lots of things. We are Anonymous. Your name, sir?"

"You're right," I said. "I was fired, but I really am Rowsdower. Aaron N. Rowsdower."

"Really?" Fawkes asked leaning forward slightly.

"Yes, really."

"Huh. The fuck was Gladstone going on about with your teeth?"

Everyone, including me, laughed, and suddenly there was a peace about the room that had been lacking. 4chan was proud of itself for being funny again.

"It's actually Gladstone that has brought me here," I said. "May I ask . . . I know this is *Anonymous* and all, but are you Quiffmonster42?"

Mumbling and gossip spread around me like ticket scalpers working a crowd outside MSG.

"Silence!" Fawkes commanded, even if his voice was a little too high to sell such a directive. "No, we have not seen Quiffmonster around these parts for quite some time. He has been distant. There have been rumors."

"What kind of rumors?"

"I'm sorry. We can't share that with an outsider."

Margo stood up. "Who are you?" she asked. "And why are you talking that way? 'Outsider'? Any 4chan member I've met in the past would have called Rowsdower a 'newfag' and then chided him for getting all 'butthurt' if he took offense. I mean, wasn't that the case when Gladstone came in here?"

"I'm sorry," Fawkes said. "Would you be more comfortable if we all shouted, 'TGTFO'?"

I looked at Margo, confused, and she whispered, "Tits or get the fuck out."

"That's not what I'm talking about," Margo said.

"Hey, baby," Fawkes continued, "you should smile more. And/or don't."

"What's that?" Margo asked, and the whole crowd replied in unison: "Schrödinger's catcall!" then burst into laughter. Without question, this was the most fun 4chan had had in months. They were delighted by the fresh meat to tool on.

"Ma'am," Fawkes continued as the room settled down, "we are not just one thing. We have no real leader, and though I'm standing onstage, I have no real power. But yes, I have the mic tonight and I don't care so much for racier jokes and language. Maybe that's the difference.

"Or maybe it's because I happen to know those two guys over in the corner, dressed as Doctor Who number seven and Doctor Who number nine? They've been here every Tuesday night for the last year. They're in love and totally fucking each other."

"He's just called 'The Doctor'!" one of them shouted. "Not Doctor Who!"

"Whatever," Fawkes said with a laugh. "You get my point, gaylord"

"Timelord!" the other corrected with a laugh, and Fawkes chuckled too, before pointing to the opposite corner. "And that woman over there in the giant peacock glasses is a regular too. I don't know. Maybe that makes it a little harder to be an asshole when you almost see the same person every week, but I will say this: You're the one who came into our home and started barking orders with no authority recognized by this organization or any organization, so I'm pretty sure if anyone's been rude, it's you two."

"You're right," Margo said. "I apologize, but as you say, Anonymous is not any one thing, and we've been told some of you are not to be trusted."

"I'm sure that's true," he said. "You trust everyone in the government? The Vatican? The police? There are always people who can't be trusted."

"It's worse in the dark," I said.

"Is it?" he asked. "Even in broad daylight, everything you can see hides something you cannot."

Like Leonards back in L.A. I'd been given another gift that made nothing more clear. But there wasn't much time to ponder, because he spoke again. "How is Gladstone?" he asked.

Margo took over as she did with Neville. "What do you want to know?" she asked.

"Friend or foe?" he asked.

"I guess that depends what side you're on," she said. "His mission statement might be different from yours. He's not doing it for the lulz."

Margo explained later that that was the mantra for many of the /b/tards, something far too trivial for our work. Fawkes did not engage the dig. He just waited a beat to reply, "Tell me anything you think will help, however you define help."

"Well," Margo said, "I can tell you Gladstone believes in pure things." She then set out the dollar-store narrative about the poor, young father and his three small girls. A story she could not tell without getting personally affected. But this was the second time I'd heard the story, so I was thinking more about my father. And my pure things.

When I was thirteen, he rented a cabin in Kinderhook, New York, where we'd stayed ten years before. We were still a family then and I was little more than a baby. In some ways, I remember the earlier trip better. I remember the green lake and gas lanterns. I remember the wooden floorboards of the five and ten in town, where my mother found a flotation device that was little more than rounded Styrofoam with a hole and a tiny fabric seat for baby legs to dangle through. No one would sell such a floating lawsuit today, but in 1973 it wasn't a problem.

I floated out into the lake alone, my mother and father arguing in the rowboat they were trying to get off the pier. I'm sure I was only yards away, but it was the farthest I'd ever been from safety. The water was dark and so dense with algae that I couldn't see what was brushing against my legs. I floated farther and farther from my parents, among hidden things that could only be felt. I would have been afraid, but I had no precedent for that. Nothing in my baby mind believed my mother would let me come to harm. I kicked my chubby legs and twisted, spinning my floaty to all sides of the lake. I got better at it. With a little work, I could get it to face any way I wanted, but I couldn't stop myself from drifting farther away. Right there, in my baby hat and sunglasses, I got my first taste of growing up, learning some things could not be controlled. But before the panic of living alone on the other side of the lake set in, my father brought the boat close enough for my mother to scoop me up and into her arms. I remember sitting in her lap. She squeezed me tight from behind as I dripped all over her jeans and watched my father's strong forearms tame the lake.

The second trip was different. My mom was home in Queens because my dad, who hadn't lived with us for two years, wanted to spend some more time with me. He never got the hang of divorce. Coming from a time that didn't believe in it, he didn't know how to worry about my homework and meals every other weekend. He just wanted to be my father. That meant the big stuff. Life lessons. So he rented the cabin for the weekend to teach me to fish.

We sat in the rowboat at six a.m., probably the same boat he and my mother had argued in a decade earlier, but this time the only Styrofoam on the lake was sitting next to him, filled with mud and worms. He showed me how to tie a hook to my line with his thick fingers threading the loop almost like a magic trick, and I followed.

"Good," he said, and pulled back the plastic from his bait. He was born and raised in the Bronx, not the bayou, so I can't imagine he'd done this too many times before, but he found his worm without flinching, even when it curled around his finger. Even when he pierced it three separate times on his hook. And especially when whatever part of a worm that's supposed to be on the inside leaked out.

"It doesn't feel it," he said. "You want me to do yours?" I knew it wasn't a question.

"No. I'll do it," I said, and plucked a worm, thinking my father's resolve must be living somewhere inside me too. I didn't flinch when the worm suddenly twisted around my finger or when I first pierced it through my hook either. Trapped at one end, the worm suddenly wrapped the rest of its body around the hook for me, and I thought perhaps I was done. After all, my bait was a much neater-looking package than the three-time-speared mess on my father's hook.

"If you leave it like that," he said, "he'll get away as soon as he hits the water."

The worm stayed tight and twisted and I hoped my father would change his mind, but then it dropped and dangled.

"I got it," my father said, and pierced the other end through my hook again, sparing me the job.

We sat and fished. Sometimes I caught him looking at me when he thought I wasn't, and I noticed him relax more and more with each moment that passed. Looking back, I understand it now. He'd created another fatherly moment. Build a snowman, go fishing, change a tire. These milestones brought relief, not because they were chores that were finally finished but because he'd gotten the chance to do them. He saw the moments enter me, and each one was proof he was still my father, and always would be. Occasionally, he'd sip from his cold coffee, relishing every sip.

"Is there anything you wanted to tell me, Dad?" I asked.

"Are you having fun?" he asked.

"Sure," I said, but that was the wrong word. It wasn't fun; it was good. It was my pure thing.

I felt a tug and heard a terrible clicking on my line until I could fight it back to my starting position.

"Reel him in," my dad said. "But not too fast."

This was definitely a bite and not a patch of seaweed or sticks. The fish pulled and changed direction, and I saw my father watch me and let me struggle myself, fighting every instinct he had to grab the pole.

"You can do this, Aaron," he said, and when the line went slack for a moment, I gained more than I lost.

"Good!" he shouted, so loud that I was lucky there was a fish on my hook because every single other one in the lake was now scared off. "Lift!"

I pulled back on my pole and my dad scooped the sunny with a net he'd brought. The fish flopped and bucked, slapping its body in the rusty boat's floor water until my dad trapped it with his foot. I looked for the hook in its mouth, but it wasn't there, and when I pulled the line his whole body moved.

"He swallowed the hook," my father said, grabbing his knife from the tackle box.

"How do we get it out?" I asked, imagining everything inside the fish coming out along with the hook if we pulled.

"We don't," my father said, and drove his knife right into the top of the fish's head. Its body fell instantly still. Its suffering was over.

My father put his hand on my shoulder. "It's official," he said. "You caught a fish."

The fish, dirty and still, seemed somehow smaller.

"Well," my father said. "I think that's enough for our first day. You want to row back to the cabin or should I?"

I didn't answer. I just took the oars and brought us

home as surely and steadily as I could while I watched my dad finish his coffee and smile about another thing his boy had learned to do.

Margo finished the story so convincingly it was hard to believe she wasn't one of those three small girls, and when she was done, others were affected too. The sound of shifting rubber and plastic bounced around the corners of the room as some of the /b/tards adjusted their masks to wipe their tears. And of course, there was also a die-hard contingent of assholes who coughed out "gay" or "lame" while burying anything good in corrosive snickers. Fawkes's reaction was harder to read because he excelled at stillness. I could be still too.

"So," I said, as dispassionately as possible, "as you say, Anonymous is not any one thing. If possible, we'd like to meet with you in private. We have a mission from Gladstone."

Fawkes took us into the shitty backstage "green room" we'd known from Gladstone's journal. We sat in folding chairs while Fawkes sat on a torn leather couch with Converse sneakers sticking out from beneath his robe. And now that we were closer, I could tell from his hands and the tiny bit of revealed skin behind the Guy Fawkes eyehole, this member of Anonymous was black.

I had interrogated countless suspects in my twenty years. It's what I did better than anyone. My information panned out. My confessions stuck. Good interrogating was all about striking a balance that came easy to me. When I was a little boy, my father told me there'd be hell to pay if he ever heard I started a fight or ran away from one. That set me on a narrow path to never be a bully or a victim. And I walked it even when interrogating suspects. But in those cases, there was a crime. I had facts. I had puzzles to solve. All I had in front of me now was a man in a mask and no authority to remove it. And the only information I was trying to gather was could this man be trusted? I wasn't sure how to do that.

I told him Gladstone was alive but not where to find him (especially since I didn't know). I told him I believed Gladstone was falsely accused of any involvement regarding the destruction of the Hollywood sign or the murder of his wife, but that could hardly be news to Anonymous. Only Senator Bramson used Gladstone as a talking point anymore, and her Republican campaign for president was desperate for any coverage as Burke hogged the media spotlight. The collective of Democratic senators and governors slowly entering the race one by one barely mentioned the Net for fear of seeming traitorous to the current administration. A former NSA head, Marvin Tandry (someone I never even dealt with during my time on the task force), was trying to build a campaign on his ability to "rout out cyberterrorism," but with zero name recognition, he was hardly making headlines. And the government was decidedly silent about Gladstone, content to let the world forget he existed. After all, they already had two people in jail for the Hollywood-sign terrorism act that had produced no fatalities, and his wife's murder was not national news. Indeed, the most incriminating piece of evidence against Gladstone was the fact he'd run away.

Fawkes didn't say a word, but I liked how he listened to me. He listened like an innocent man. When I paused to consider my next step, he spoke: "Are you trying to ask for our help, Mr. Rowsdower?"

"Yes, but I don't know if you're trustworthy."

"Well, in these times, the man in a mask is the only one you can trust."

"That's a cute line for a Batman movie," I said, "but I used to be a fed. Know who wears masks? Criminals."

"What's the assignment?" he asked.

There were no facts. Only what born-agains call faith and I call gut, but I trusted him, and I told him that there might be a way to get recorded proof of the Hollywood-sign bombing and that this proof would, according to Gladstone, show Tobey and Jeeves played no role in it.

"You want our hackers on it?" he said.

"I guess I do."

"I think I'll be able to find more than a few people interested in that assignment when the Net returns to-morrow, Agent Rowsdower."

"I'm not an agent anymore. Remember?"

"Sure you are," he said. "Now you're an agent of Anonymous."

Report 6

We rode the train back to Bayside. Margo was happy, but I didn't feel like talking. I'd lost control again, untethered to a job, I might as well have been splashing in my floaty as I went from L.A. to New York to London and back again. Worse yet, I was taking orders from Gladstone and waiting on another letter to find out where to go next.

In the beginning it had been about self-preservation. Gladstone had gotten a raw deal and so had I. I assumed the two were linked and both involved the Apocalypse. And while I still believed that, after months of looking for him, we were pen pals at best.

"Do you think I could crash at your place one more night?" Margo asked. "I'm catching a plane in the morning."

The conductor was coming, and I took out my ticket,

realizing that even months after being fired, I was still paying for my monthly mail and ride.

"Where are you going?" I asked Margo. She wasn't quick to answer, but then I remembered her crush Down Under. "Oh, Australia," I said. "Well, have fun jumping your miner."

Margo let the conductor punch her ticket and move on before speaking. "Thanks," she said. "Now the train guy thinks I'm fucking minors."

I tried to smile even though I didn't feel like it. Part of me was angry because I thought Margo was being frivolous taking an Australian vacation in the middle of an investigation. Another part was jealous, and that was getting harder to conceal.

"Sure thing," I said. "Will you need a ride to the airport?"

The next morning, I watched C-SPAN while Margo showered. Hamilton Burke was having a town hall meeting in Iowa. He'd lost the suit and the vest, and now was wearing a white shirt with the sleeves rolled up, along with his red tie and leather suspenders.

"Good people of Iowa," he said. "Thank you for joining me here today, as we continue our efforts to make America work."

The crowd was enthusiastic, but slightly more tempered than in New York. Burke would need to do more than change clothes to gain their respect. He continued on with a modified version of his Federal Hall speech about the promise of America and people working too hard for too little. It resonated, particularly the part when

he described America as a broken business no true businessman would stand for. But when it came to discuss-
ing the Internet, it was different. Not only because there
were no potshots taken at Gladstone, or even a mention
of him, but because the Net was about to return.

"And now my friends, speaking of what's broken, let's
turn to the Internet. It's been nearly one year in this
Apocalypse. The most important resource of the twenty-
first century has been kept out of the hands of the people
for twelve months. And I wish I could tell you it was just
this administration's incompetence. It's not—although
there's surely plenty of incompetence."

There were some knowing chuckles, and Burke found
where they were coming from. "That's right. It *is* laugh-
able," he said, pointing to some of his new friends. "Remember their health-care website? Ridiculous. I've had
to set up lots of websites for my various businesses and
enterprises, and let me tell you, when I hire someone to
do something, it gets done.

"But there are bigger problems. It seems very curious
to me that the government can only return the Net to us,
to the people . . . once they get their hands on it. And
now, wouldn't you know it? Once the government has
gotten involved, it comes with extra charges. *Of course it
does.*"

Burke surveyed the room, making sure everyone was
where they were supposed to be. They were.

"And who says it ends there?" Burke asked. "This fee.
This government control. I tell you right now, this is
just the starting point. You watch. Suddenly, sites critical
to the administration won't load as fast. More blackouts
will occur when the government feels communications

need to be cut. But don't despair, because this administration, indeed no administration, can truly take away our Internet, and do you know why?"

He kept scanning the room, seeing more and more and more pleased voters.

"The government can't take the Internet from the people because the Internet *is* people. The Internet is you and me. All of us. *And we're still here!*"

There it was again. The phrase that had been spray-painted on the wall of the Veterans' Affairs Building under Gladstone's Wi-Fi symbol the day I was fired. One of the Messiah Movement's many graffiti slogans had been co-opted by a billionaire running for president, and the crowd loved it, erupting into guttural roars that increasingly grounded the higher-pitched cheers.

"It doesn't matter what's done to us," Burke continued. "We the people can take anything. We the people find a way."

He turned reflective and soft for a moment. "Y'know," he said, "about twenty years ago, I was in upstate New York, surveying a mall for purchase, and I saw something I'll never forget. It was a young father. He couldn't have been more than thirty, but he had three daughters, maybe ten, eight, and six years old, and they were all heading to a dollar store. He didn't have fancy clothes or a fancy haircut. There was paint splattered on his ripped jeans, but as they got to the entrance, all three little girls stopped and looked back at their dad, awaiting his permission. They had respect, y'see, and this father threw up his hands like a king and said, 'OK, girls, you can have anything you want!'

"And as I watched these girls shriek and run into the store like little princesses, I realized this man was a hero. With so little to give, he made his girls feel spoiled, because people can do that. We can do that. We can wade through all the garbage and lies that comes out of DC, all the filth that creeps into our daily lives, and make something pure. Something pure for ourselves and those we love. My name is Hamilton Burke, and I want you to help me do just that. For all of us in this country. God bless you, and God bless America!"

Burke had stolen Gladstone's pure thing. The story I had now heard Margo twice tell. Had Gladstone told him? Had Margo? There was too much I didn't know and it made me angry. Back on the job, incidents came with facts, and then there was forensics, there were witnesses. I was tired with this puzzle. No databases, no interrogation rooms, and no gun.

I went to the guest room. Margo was still in the shower, and I could hear the water running. Her luggage was open on the bed, and I paused for a moment. This was a violation, but I had grilled Gladstone, Oz, Tobey, Jeeves, Leonards, and Neville. I even questioned Anonymous as best I could, but what had I asked of Margo? She told me only what I knew and dug as much as she revealed. Worse yet, I'd let her get away with it like some rookie cop with a crush. And in return, she'd delivered marching orders from Gladstone, made sure I did my duty, and then flew back to some asshole in Australia.

I went through her luggage looking for something to hold on to. At first, I saw a few pairs of underwear and pushed them out of the way without pausing or really looking, because I was an asshole not a pervert. And then

I found something. Letters. Some originals on paper and some photocopies, to and from her Australian lover-boy miner. Some prick named Parker. I listened to make sure the water was still running and then I read them, telling myself it was necessary for the investigation. But it wasn't, because they weren't clues. They were love letters. And not mere sexts moved to paper or invitations to a good time. I wasn't so angry that I couldn't recognize love, and I was old enough to remember what it looked like on paper. The originals were his and, for some reason, she must have photocopied her replies before sending them off.

It was an instant and obvious love. It didn't grow over the course of the letters; they just revealed more and more of it to each other.

Dear Margo,

You left just hours ago and I already miss you. I want to say I'm not sure how I ever lived without you, but I'm doing that now. And I'm alive. But living's harder now that I know you exist. I wish I could describe my love in a way that doesn't sound like pain and need, because that's not love and it's not why I love you.

I love your tiny face in my hands, and your long arms around me. I love how your shoes fall off because your feet are too skinny. I didn't know you were what I was looking for. "Oh, OK, 5' 10" chicks with long legs and short dirty-blond hair is your type." I know that's stupid. I know you'd be you even if you were 5' 5" and brunette, but part of me says, "OK, that! You love that!" as if all of you is wrapped up in one package. I just think

*that's my stupid brain's way of saying I love all of you,
unconditionally.*

*I can't wait to see you again. I love everything you do
for me and the only thing better would be being able to
do for you.*

Love,
Parker

P.S. I have not taken off the David Bowie The Man
Who Fell to Earth *fedora for more than a few minutes
since you gave it to me. I know, you said you had all sorts
of movie memorabilia from your Marty days, but of all
the things to have, this is just the greatest gift you could
give. Better than a lightsaber.*

Oh Parker,
*I'm glad you like the hat. It suits you. And I'm happy you
like it better than a lightsaber, because that's one thing I
definitely can't get for you. I might have a line on Lou
Ferrigno's codpiece from* Hercules? *Does that do anything for you?*

*Also, you do a lot more for me than you know. Before
you, I was living in a world of diminished expectations.
And now I think maybe I made it to my mid-thirties
without ever knowing anyone. I stayed an arm's length
away because closeness brought disappointment. But I
gobble you up, and I can't get close enough to you.*

*I will come see you again soon, but maybe we should
talk about things. I know you just started a new job, but
I don't think me setting up Prague Rock Productions in
Bumblefuck, Australia, makes sense, and with all the*

stuff I'm doing to make my movie work, I can't buy Aus plane tickets indefinitely. I love you. I can't stop saying it. I love you. See you soon.

Love, Margo

P.S. I love you.
P.P.S. Shut up.

I looked for more, but that seemed to be the last of the correspondence, and then, even though the water was still running, I heard the bathroom door open. Margo entered the room in a towel and found me standing beside her open luggage.

"Burke just told Gladstone's dollar-store story on TV," I said.

"You've been through my luggage," she said.

"How does Burke know Gladstone's story?"

"I don't know. Why don't you ask Gladstone?" she asked, securing her towel, and looking to see if anything had been taken.

"I'd like to," I said. "That's why I'm looking for him, instead of running off to Australia," I said.

Margo pulled back on the netting of her case, where I'd hastily shoved the letters.

"You read my letters," she said. "Who do you think you are? The NET Recovery Act's over, Agent Rowsdower."

"Oh, you know who I am. I haven't hidden anything. You're the one who's a mystery. That's the problem. I let you into my investigation, into my apartment, and I don't know a thing about you."

"And that gives you the right to go through my shit?"

I didn't answer, and she grabbed some clothes from her suitcase with her left hand while she kept the right tight at the top of the towel.

"I needed to know if I was being played," I said.

"And that's how you went about it? Fuck you."

She headed back to the bathroom but stopped after a few steps. "Tell me. How am I playing you? What did you discover besides what kind of underwear I own?"

"That you're in love."

"Is that a crime?"

"No, it's not a crime," I said, and tried to soften my tone. "Look, I get it. From everything I know and everything I've seen, I'm the asshole."

"Oh, good, so it's agreed!"

"But I also know you haven't told me everything. I still believe that. So tell me what I don't know."

"I have no idea how Burke knows Gladstone's dollar-store thing, but instead of putting your paws on my love letters and panties, you might want to accuse Neville? We told him days ago."

"Let me ask you another question."

"What?"

"Why is the water still running?"

"Because I've been living out of a suitcase for days, and I'm steaming my dress. Now, if the interrogation is over, I'll be going," she said, and she did.

It was the second time Margo had left me in anger, and even though I'd been wrong on both occasions, I also knew each departure was preceded by my attempts to pierce beyond the surface. Sure, I was jealous, but not all of this was schoolboy bullshit. There were things I hadn't discovered. Things she hid with what she offered: jokes,

information . . . she even hid with kindness. I couldn't
see everything I needed. Some things had to be felt.

The good news is the new Internet came back the day
she left. With no job, no Margo, and no idea what to do
next, I saddled up to my crappy Dell so I could click, re-
fresh, and "investigate" without leaving my chair. I had
an email from my cable provider explaining the additional governmental fee I'd be seeing on my bill. It gave
estimates of the kind of expenses we could expect, and
the downloading of content was monetized like in the
old AOL days. Simply being online carried only a small
charge, but that amount times all of America was a hell
of a lot of money.

The next few days went quickly, filled with Chinese
takeout, pizza delivery, and periodic 7-Eleven beer runs.
For the first time in literally years, I went four days without shaving, and my stubble came in gray at the side-
burns and the tip of my chin. I wondered how long it had
been waiting beneath my skin, and when I would have
first noticed it if I hadn't faithfully shaved every morning. I even shaved on weekends so I wouldn't be slowed
down Monday mornings with that snagging two-day
growth.

Now that I was no longer keeping FBI hours, I decided to get a laptop so I could take my investigation to bed.
Soon after, I woke to a story on Anonymous. They were
back in business. Mission accomplished. Not only had
they hacked into the Hollywood sign's surveillance server
and obtained the footage of the explosion, they'd put it
online. Multiple cameras playing at once showed Gladstone, Jeeves, and Tobey hiding from the spotlight of a

black helicopter before splitting up. An incredibly disheveled Gladstone, wearing the hat I now owned, ran down the hill with a metal box while Tobey and Jeeves headed in the opposite direction. And then the most compelling part, some sort of charge fired from the helicopter, exploding the *D* in "HOLLYWOOD." A helicopter and fire from above, just like the neighbor reports on the murder of Gladstone's ex, Romaya Petralia.

The footage ended with a man in a Guy Fawkes mask—possibly the guy from the Bowery Club, although the voice had been distorted—saying, "The three men in this video are Wayne Gladstone, Brendan Tobey, and Dan 'Jeeves' McCall. Right now, Tobey and Jeeves sit in a detention center for this act of vandalism they clearly did not commit. They have not been charged for these crimes under any valid form of due process, but are merely being held, indefinitely and without legal counsel, at the Veterans' Affairs Building in Los Angeles, under this government's NET Recovery Act. The whereabouts of Gladstone, also known as the Internet Messiah, are unknown, likely in hiding for this crime he clearly did not commit. Anonymous does not know the affiliation of that black helicopter responsible for the destruction, but we will. Anonymous is not directly affiliated with Mr. Gladstone, but we hope he is safe, and we want him to come home."

I wanted to talk to Margo. I wanted to talk to Gladstone, but I had no way of speaking to either, so I just kept refreshing the news, watching the story get bigger and bigger. I thought about paying a second visit to Tobey and Jeeves, but now that I had no connection to the

FBI, there'd be no way to do that. Also, there was no reason to think that would be helpful. While Tobey had been obstinate, Jeeves struck me as somewhat unhinged.

I had paid him a visit on my way back from LAX, Gladstone's bloody hat still in hand. I wanted information. I wanted to know where Gladstone was and why he ran. I thought a bloody hat might shake Jeeves up, and it did, but not exactly the way I wanted. I entered his cell, which was just a converted office at the Veterans' Affairs Building with the windows boarded up. He was sitting on his cot with his eyes closed, his prison blues mostly covering his gut.

"Daniel McCall," I said, deliberately rough.

"Just Dan McCall," he said. "My name is Dan. But please, call me Jeeves." He kept his eyes closed, and that really pissed me off, so I threw Gladstone's hat onto his lap. It startled him. Twice. Not just the impact of the landing, but the sense impression he seemed to catch off it.

"Gladstone?" he asked, eyes suddenly fully open.

"Not quite," I said, and pulled a seat up to his cot before sitting down on it backwards. "I'm Special Agent Rowsdower."

"Really?"

"Yes."

"But your teeth—"

"I know," I said. "Your boy Gladstone did a number on me in his little book."

"Is he all right?" Jeeves asked.

"I don't know."

"Is this his blood?" he asked, holding up the hat.

"Look, I didn't come here to answer your questions, I—"

Just then, Jeeves reached forward quicker than I thought he could and grabbed my right hand. My training brought me to my feet with my left fist cocked. It wasn't as solid as my right, but I was pretty sure it could stop a librarian. I'd jab his cheek. No reason to break his nose, I thought, but then he spoke.

"You're having it tested," he said, and I dropped my fist. "You think it's Romaya's. Someone's killed Gladstone's ex-wife."

I sat down, taking my hand back from Jeeves. "Now, Mr. McCall, how would you possibly know that unless Gladstone told you he was going to do it or . . . you did it?"

Jeeves wanted to laugh, but he looked like he was seeing Romaya's dead body as I had, so it ended in kind of a choked cough and left something distasteful in his mouth. "You don't really believe that," he said.

"How else?" I asked.

"Well, for one, I'm a psychic, remember? And two, please don't pull that G-man stuff on me. I've held your hand. You don't believe I've hurt anyone. You don't believe Gladstone's hurt anyone, and you're not hunting him like a criminal. You want to know who killed his wife. You want to know what's going on. And you want something more."

"What's that?" I asked.

"I'm not sure," he said, "but would you do me a favor, please, Special Agent Rowsdower?"

"Get you out of this holding cell and into some form of due process?" I asked.

"Well, that will be nice," he said with a real smile this time, "but something else first. Would you please put this hat on for me?"

"Why?"

"Please?"

I took Gladstone's fedora and placed it on my head. Jeeves smiled the way men do when their hope is rescued before spoiling.

"What?" I asked.

"I think you *will* get me out of here, Agent Rowsdower," he said. "Not today. But you will."

And now, months later, it was in motion. In the days that followed Anonymous's release of the footage, scores of its members, along with Internet Reclamation Movement members, showed up to protest outside the Veterans' Affairs Building. The Net was back, but the people were still united, and there seemed to be more of them than ever, because Gladstone's book continued to spread. It was hard to tell who was who. There were guys in black with Guy Fawkes masks and there were lots of people in Gladstone masks too, Margo's soft launch was certainly helping the cause. There was no way to say who was who, and of course there were people with no costumes and some just in fedoras and jackets. There was also new graffiti on the wall outside the building. Right where Gladstone's Wi-Fi symbol once stood, there were calls to FREE TOBEY AND JEEVES and BRING GLADSTONE HOME.

The next day, I made a point of staying out of my apartment. Aside from some runs to the local CVS, 7-Eleven, and liquor store, I'd barely been out for weeks. I had told myself this was my vacation. My time to make up for all those personal days I never took over a twenty-year career. But I'd grown a beard. I'd put on at least five pounds. I didn't look like me, and it was enough. I used to wake up refreshed at six a.m. on seven hours' sleep, but now it took all my strength to get out the door by ten. My khakis were getting tight, and I traded them for a looser pair of old jeans.

I started my day with a shave and haircut at the barber I'd gone to once a month for the last ten years. Even after I got fired, I still kept going on weekends like a workingman so I didn't have to talk about why I wasn't at the office. Today was Tuesday, and I hadn't seen Vincent in about two months.

"Aaron! Come in," he said, swatting at his chair with the white towel he kept over his left shoulder. "I barely recognize you. No work today?"

"Morning, Vinnie," I said, taking the chair. "I'm on vacation."

Vinnie took good care of me. Hot towel, straight razor, the whole deal. He ran his knife like a pro, and then he buzzed the sides and back really tight. All those new gray hairs fell away into little geriatric tumbleweeds, or were now so short they disappeared. I stared at myself in the mirror as Vinnie combed my hair up top, readying it for cutting. The weight I'd gained had softened my face. I looked less hungry.

"OK," Vinnie said. "What about the top? Same as usual?" he said, making a part. My hair was only about an inch longer than usual, but it was the longest it had ever been, and with the buzzed sides and back it looked even longer.

"Leave it," I said.

"Leave it?" Vinnie asked, flipping the length back and

forth with his comb so it flopped around like basset-hound ears.

"Yeah, I think so," I said.

"You'll look like one of the hipster douchebag kids," he said, and I laughed.

"Yeah, let's go for that," I said. "Time for a change."

I left Vinnie's holding Gladstone's fedora in my hand so I could sport my new cut as I walked Bell Boulevard in my sports jacket and jeans. The only thing keeping me from falling down a Gladstone hole was that I didn't have a flask on me. I headed north to the shopping center, watching the world work again. The traffic lights were humming, and kids in the stores were on their phones walking with their heads down.

The shopping-center bookstore was now selling a version of Gladstone's journal for a dollar. They'd dressed it up nicely with a strategically lo-fi cardstock cover. I bought one and noticed no publisher was listed. I doubted this was another part of Margo's soft launch. More likely she had a lawsuit on her hands, considering she now owned the rights. I wanted to tell her, but had no way to reach her. We met when the Net was down, and given the state of her departure, we didn't stop to trade emails. I didn't even have her cell. And even if I did, would I really want to hear the sounds of some Aussie asshole shifting around in the background?

So I walked back down Bell Boulevard. The important thing, it seemed, was to keep moving. That's what they say, right? This too shall pass, and all of that. I put my hat back on and walked until I hit some miserable sports bar near Northern. It seemed a good choice. On a Tuesday afternoon, a dive bar would be filled with vagrant drunks, but a sports bar had a better chance of housing workingmen. Guys in construction or non-9-to-5 office jobs like my dad used to have. I needed to surround myself with men who wouldn't be a depressing mirror. So I sat at the bar, ordered a Bud, and watched the Mets. Or at least looked at the TV like I was watching the Mets. My Bronx father had wanted me to be a Yankee fan. I put my fedora on the bar, and remembered it wasn't mine. It wasn't even Gladstone's. It was his grandfather's. I did a little math, factored in Gladstone's Judaism, and concluded the owner of the hat was probably a Brooklyn Dodgers fan. Great. The gang was all here.

As I predicted, the bar was filled with construction workers who'd just gotten off a shift. They were dirty and tired, and, as far as I could tell, they were happy. Why not? They'd finished the day's work, and they probably all knew what tomorrow held. The senior guys, at least, had guaranteed spots, but the younger guys would get there too. If they kept their mouths shut and did what they were told. They'd secure spots. Get the sweet gigs where they'd just watch for an incoming rogue train while two other men soldered a new bolt to the tracks. They noticed the hat. They noticed my hair. They didn't say anything.

I finished my Bud and ordered another because it seemed more productive than going back home. And then channel 9 went to a commercial and some local news anchor I'd never seen teased the evening news: "The Hollywood sign bombers go free. News at six!" It went back to the game, but I wasn't waiting.

"Turn it to CNN, please?" I asked the bartender, a late-thirties single mom, sporting chipped red nail polish, dyed blond hair, and an official bar T-shirt tied in a cleavage-sporting knot. (She also wore an open-heart locket around her neck with a pic of her and another one of her son cut and taped to each side. Plus no wedding ring. I was still on the job.) She reached for the remote reflexively in response to my directive, but then turned to the construction workers. They were regulars.

"We're watching the game, buddy," the oldest one said. He was about my age. Thirty extra pounds, but slathered on top of a muscled interior developed over years of hauling drywall and cable.

If I were still who I used to be, I would have flashed a badge and declared the television part of official business. Or maybe I would have moved in such a way that my jacket would pull back and reveal my gun. But I didn't have those options. "This will just take a second," I said. "It's important."

The bartender looked back at him for his ruling, but it wasn't going well so I just took the remote from her hand and changed the channel myself. "Sorry," I said. "Just a second," I repeated to her, and I was right. CNN was already deep into the story.

"Today, the NSA released Brendan Tobey and Dan 'Jeeves' McCall from detention. The two had been held under the NET Recovery Act since last December as suspects in the bombing of the famous Hollywood sign in Los Angeles."

The camera cut to footage of Tobey and Jeeves both being escorted out of the Veteran's Affairs Building. They were thinner than when I'd seen them last, but they were happy. Jeeves had an almost Zen-like contentment as he was pushed through a huge crowd of protesters cheering his release. There was every kind of person in the crowd: Anonymous, Messiah Movement devotees, fans of Gladstone's book, and, of course, normal people too.

Tobey, flanked by NSA on both sides, searched the crowd so intently I wondered if he was looking for an assassin. Then he shouted, "Come to Santa Monica tonight! I'll be on Tinder! God bless the Internet!"

My burly friend had had enough. "That's enough," he said. "I'm giving you one chance to put the game back on."

I raised the "one second" finger of my left hand while continuing to hold the remote. I was intent on catching the final words of this story. I even tilted the remote toward the bar TV, indicating the story's importance. My old L.A. supervisor, Patrick Dunican, was onscreen wearing a black suit and aviator sunglasses while giving a statement. Dunican was from New York like me. NSA had tapped him first and he was only too happy to go out there. L.A. weather afforded more opportunities to wear his sunglasses, no doubt. And then he tapped me to follow him—faithful employee I was.

My construction-worker friend wasn't impressed with the news, and moved in even closer until our eyes were inches apart. His left shoulder dug into the right side of my chest as he positioned his body for a right hook.

"I'd shove that remote right up your ass," he said, "but I think you'd like it too much, ya half a fag."

This haircut was really doing wonders for me.

"Who told you?" I asked with faux outrage. "Unless . . . was that you manning the glory hole at Penn Station?"

I wished Margo were here for that one. She'd appreciate it, and it was about as quick as I could be. With jokes anyway. My reflexes were better for fighting, which was good, because he threw his right and I took half a step back, grabbing a fist of his thick, greasy black hair and redirecting his own momentum as I slammed his head into the bar. And then again. And one more time. I had to do three. He had friends I couldn't take. This was a statement. I let him fall and stared at his buddies.

"I'm watching the end of this, got it?"

I had been distracted, but Dunican was asked if Tobey and Jeeves's release meant "The Internet Messiah" also was no longer a suspect in the Hollywood sign or any other bombing.

"If by that you mean Wayne Gladstone," Dunican said, "he is not a suspect in this investigation."

I threw a twenty on the bar and turned my back on the three men who meant me harm as I headed for the door. Four, actually, but one wouldn't be in any shape to do much of anything for a while. Quickening my pace would mean fear, and fear would mean I was ripe for attack. I walked extra-slow, but I snuck a glance in one of the beer-logo mirrors on the wall as I straightened my hat to make sure I was safe. But even when I got outside I kept walking. I felt something chasing me.

I wasn't sure where the panic was coming from. The NSA had publicly declared that Gladstone wasn't a suspect, and while I knew better than to trust them, making such a statement seemed needlessly declarative if they really were in pursuit. And I had to admit that despite my termination and predictions, even thirteen months into the Apocalypse no one was after me either.

Plus, the Internet had returned, sort of. But I still kept walking faster and faster, positive I was being chased. Not by my job, because I didn't have one. And not by my investigation.

I headed north again back to the Bay Terrace shopping center, until I caught my reflection in the Uncle Jack's Steakhouse window. Maybe it was the sun or the warping of the glass but it reflected like a funhouse mirror. I was shorter, wider. Nothing drastic, just enough to make me not me, and I realized who was chasing me. Gladstone was in the glass, staring back.

I knew I had to go. I didn't even want to hit my apartment before leaving, but I needed a passport and luggage. I packed a bag as quickly as I could, not even stopping to take a leak. I'd piss at the airport. The important thing was getting out while I still could. I threw three handfuls of clothes and my laptop into my suitcase and walked to the taxi service on the corner.

We hit the road and I watched Bayside get farther away. I connected my iPhone to my laptop like I had not yet done, and got online. I was fully aware that running off to Australia to find some girl made me just as much like Gladstone as staying in my apartment and getting drunk, but at least I wouldn't be alone.

"Where you going?" my driver asked.

"JFK," I said.

"I know," he replied, "but which terminal? What airline?"

"Oh," I said. "Not sure yet. I'm going to Australia."

"Qantas? Virgin?"

"Either," I said. "They both go to Australia, right?" I continued my investigation. Wherever Margo was, she was with her miner, and my invasion of her privacy had given me a name even if it sounded cartoonishly fake: Parker Lawrence. I had about twenty minutes before we hit the airport. I searched Australian records, driver's licenses, censuses, anything I could that had a name. Nothing hit at first, and then I found him. On Twitter, no less. His avi was merely the site's default egg, and he'd only tweeted a few times, but it was all I had. Twitter handle, @ParkerLawrence. His few tweets were only pictures of the beach. Insane blues in the water and sky, and white sand the likes of which I'd never seen at Jones Beach. He had his location settings on and I used that information to run searches with specificity, until I homed in on an exact address. We were entering JFK.

"I'm taking you to Quantas," my driver said.

"That's fine," I said.

"You figure out where you're heading?" he asked.

"I sure did," I replied with a laugh, checking the name of this particular region in Queensland for a fourth time.

"Yeah?"

"I'm going to Gladstone," I said.

Part III

Report 7

I didn't know what I'd say to Margo when I got there, and I was worried about it, but less worried than I was about staying in Queens. Traveling made me feel like I was doing something, and while I may have been laid off, I could still afford the $1,200 ticket due to my pension and savings. That was a good feeling. Of course, the quarter bottle of Johnnie Walker I swigged at JFK wasn't hurting either. In my hurry to pack, I'd thrown the remains of a bottle in a case, picturing myself unwinding with a glass in the bed of some imagined Australian hotel. Unfortunately, I'd forgotten the part about going through security with fluids, and since it was a shame to waste it, I knocked it back at the scanner. Then I settled into my buzz, keeping it at a nice smolder with periodic cocktails and laptop surfing for the rest of the day.

The next thirty or so hours, my trip from JFK to LAX

to Sydney to Brisbane to Gladstone is a bit of a blur. I remember Googling that Gladstone's main industry was mining, but it was no small Pennsylvania coal town. It looked like a resort postcard and even though June was their winter, the expected weather was in the 70s (or 20, using Celsius bullshit).

I also read complaints about the new web—and not just the fees it now carried, but glitches. Serious ones. Bank of America had closed its site temporarily and emailed all its customers not to conduct banking online while it investigated an imposter site.

Between sleeping on the long leg to Sydney, the booze, and the time change, I was completely disoriented by the time I reached Brisbane. The airport was bright and spacious like a mechanical heaven, but it had the earthly markings of KFC and Victoria's Secret. So this is what I was missing by neglecting a life of travel and leisure. Their Burger King was called Hungry Jack's, which I assumed was because crocodile hunters bow before no man. I found a bar and got a cup of coffee. It was a weird order for a bar, but I didn't particularly care about what any Australian thought of me. The American influence continued to penetrate the airport. Charlie Rose's interview show was on the bar's TV. Tobey and Jeeves were sitting side by side at Charlie's table in the darkened studio.

"Gentlemen, first I want to congratulate you on your release," Charlie said.

Jeeves was quick with a reply. "Thank you, Charlie, but that sounds like we were convicted of something. There was no crime. There was no charge. We were just held, *indefinitely*, without right to counsel, because we were 'persons of interest' under the NET Recovery Act."

"Do you think most Americans appreciate the due-process argument you're making?"

"I'm not sure," Jeeves replied. "Before the Net went down, there was no shortage of online content equating caring with foolishness. A kind of jaded and false intellectualism that mistook passion for naïveté. A culture that would give you a list of five reasons it was OK not to care instead of one essay about why things matter."

"Mr. Tobey," Charlie said, "I understand you're a bit of a blogger yourself. Do you agree with Mr. McCall?"

Tobey hadn't been listening. "Mr. McCall? Oh, Jeeves! Um, well, he certainly used a lot of big words, but I dunno. The Net's also filled with people who care about stupid shit. Oh fuck, can I say 'shit'?"

Charlie laughed. "You can't say either of those words, but we'll bleep it."

"Cool, well then let me answer that in two ways. First, fuuuuuuuuuuuuuuuuuuuuuuck, and second, I don't think most people care about the NET Recovery Act, because they feel they haven't done anything wrong, so they've got nothing to fear."

"But that's the point," Jeeves said. "What did we do that was 'wrong'?" he asked, making finger quotes.

"You mean, besides the super-gay way you just made those bunny-rabbit fingers? Nothing. We didn't deserve this. I'm not arguing that. We were held simply for being friends with Gladstone."

Charlie tried to focus the conversation. "You're talking about Wayne Gladstone, the so-called Internet Messiah, and author of the Internet Apocalypse notebook that's gone paper-viral as they say."

Tobey and Jeeves nodded.

"What can you tell me about him?" Charlie asked.

"What do you want to know?" Jeeves asked.

"Well, for one, you're the person who dubbed him the Internet Messiah. The Net is back. Is he still the Messiah? What does that even mean?"

"It's confusing," Jeeves admitted, "but I know what I saw, and I know we still need . . . actually, Charlie, do you mind if I just talk to the camera for a second? I'll be brief." Charlie nodded and Jeeves came right out of the screen. "Wayne," he said, "I'm sorry for all the hits that came your way. I'm sorry for everything, but you're still here. I feel you, and it's time to come home. We're here for you. Thank you, Charlie."

"You're welcome. Now, when you say—"

But Charlie didn't get to finish because Tobey interrupted. "Actually, Charlie, could I also beg your indulgence for a moment?"

"Go ahead," Charlie said, and the camera turned to Tobey, who then pulled a flashlight out from under his shirt and shined it around the blackened studio behind him, revealing cables, ladders, various tech equipment, and most of all, nothing of interest. But Tobey was delighted. "Whooooo! Man, I've wanted to do that for years," he said. "Kind of a cheapskate way to build a set, huh Charlie?"

It was only an hour-and-a-half flight from Brisbane to Gladstone, and when I arrived I asked the kid at the rental-car place for a GPS vehicle. I didn't trust myself to find the Love Miner's apartment without it, especially driving on the wrong side of the road.

"I could sell it to you, but it won't do you much good, mate," he said, and I tried not to smile about how Australian he sounded.

"Why not?" I asked.

"The Internet's down again, isn't it?" he said.

"Is it?"

"It surely is," he said. "Didn't last long. Where ya headed?"

I reached for the paper I'd placed in my inside pocket. "Um, four slash eighteen Quinn Lane?" I asked. "Sorry, that looks like a fraction to me, . . ."

"That just means Unit 4, 18 Quinn Lane. Townhouses. You won't need GPS, I'll draw you a map. It's like ten minutes away. Five roundabouts though. . . ."

I got into a Toyota Corolla not too different from my Honda Accord back home except that the steering wheel was on the other side. I was sober now, and that was good because I was flying blind without GPS and I took five roundabouts in quick succession like a kid at a birthday party spun round and round before being pushed toward a piñata. By the fifth roundabout I had no faith of traveling in the right direction and started looking for a service station where I might ask directions, but then I hit Trunk Street, just like I was supposed to.

"You've got to be fucking kidding me," I barked at no one. Right there, at the intersection, some asshole had planted palm trees. I couldn't imagine they were indigenous to Australia, but it was also hard to believe someone would willingly bring a little slice of L.A. into their home. The trees gave way to a string of business signage: GLADSTONE LEGAL, GLADSTONE HOLISTIC, GLADSTONE REAL ESTATE. Two more turns and I was on Quinn Lane. In one drunken, panic-infused dash, I'd gone from New York to Australia, spun five times round, and never got lost even driving down the wrong side of the road. Maybe Gladstone was on to something.

I sat outside the miner's apartment in my rented Corolla without the first idea what to say. The door and windows of the two-story brick house remained closed with no signs of life inside. There was a car of the same make and model as mine parked outside the house, and I wondered if it was Margo's rental. Maybe she'd bought one by now. She was here enough.

The day was overcast, without the tropical blues and whites I'd seen on Parker's Twitter. I pictured him answering the door in a T-Shirt and jeans, after I rang the doorbell. It was hard to imagine him without a flashlight-topped miner's helmet, which I knew was absurd. I also tried to picture Margo coming out of a back room, saying, "It's OK, Parker. He's with me," but I knew that was just as ridiculous as the helmet.

I had no right to be where I was. No authority. As a soldier in the NET Recovery Act, I was used to that, but now there was no government behind me. Just me and my needs. So I sat there for an hour looking for an opening or any form of information to help me decide what to do next. There was nothing, but I'd been on stakeouts before, and I knew there was always nothing, until there was something. Besides, if this wasn't business, then I was just a stalker. This was a stakeout. Why else would I have just pissed into my empty coffee cup?

After the second hour, I caught a break. Margo came out of the bottom apartment alone, moving with a determination that I read as anger, but maybe it wasn't. Maybe her suitcase was just too heavy. Perhaps she'd added a padlock to keep out assholes like me. In any event, she was alone and heading for her car. I wouldn't get a better chance than this, and I wasn't going to let her get away.

"Margo," I called, getting out of my car while pretending my legs weren't asleep. I threw off a casual wave as if I'd merely spotted some close friend on the way to the supermarket.

She turned to the street where I was parked and popped her head forward in my direction. "What?" she asked, and that was all she said. The talking part was my obligation.

I limped toward her as casually as possible. "Going on a trip?" I asked.

"Sorry, Officer, but it's not your turn to question. What are you doing here?"

"Let's get a cup of coffee. I'll explain everything," I said, even though I had no idea what would even constitute a compelling explanation.

"What are you doing here, Aaron?" she repeated.

I looked at the house. There was no movement in the windows. I'd have to say something. She put down her suitcase and took a step away from her car and closer to me. "Aaron?"

"Well, the investigation doesn't stop just because you fly off to Australia."

We were now only a foot or so apart. "Why are you here, Aaron?"

"I couldn't take my apartment," I said, and that was the truth. It felt good.

"So you came to Australia?" she asked.

"Well, y'know, New York summers are sticky."

"Aaron."

"I didn't know where else to go, Margo."

I guess that was the right thing to say. She was touched, or maybe the anger that had pushed her from the house had returned. I wasn't sure. I was never sure with Margo. But she swallowed whatever emotion was welling up, and said, "Thank you."

"You're welcome."

She grabbed her keys and popped the trunk. "Well, as it turns out," she said, putting her bag inside, "I think I have a destination for you. Wanna go to Sydney?"

"Not really, no," I said, "I've just been there, but we can take my car. I need to return it at the airport anyway."

Margo took her suitcase out of the trunk. "Did you bring Gladstone's fedora?"

"Yeah. Why?"

"I was hoping you had something to cover that haircut. You look like a hipster douchebag."

I was too exhausted from the nonstop traveling to speak much on the plane. Besides, I wanted to give Margo her space after everything that had happened in New York. Still, I did ask her one question once we took off.

"Have you forgiven me?" I asked.

She swallowed her first response, which I'm pretty

confident was something like "I invited you to Sydney, didn't I?" and, instead, said, "What you did in New York was an invasion."

"I'm sorry."

"I know you are," she said, and smiled like I hadn't seen since the day she showed up outside my apartment. I fell asleep, and it wasn't until we landed that I realized I hadn't bothered to ask where in Sydney we were going or why.

I found that out the next morning in the car. We were off to another ICANN key holder like Neville, except this one was very famous. Reginald Stanton, the Australian entrepreneur and founder of countless companies from the now long-dead music business to airline travel to Internet providers.

"How are we going to get his attention?"

"Shouldn't be too hard," she said, pulling into an office building parking lot in the center of the CBD, which I learned stood for central business district. "He reached out to me. We have a scheduled appointment at noon."

"Seriously?" I asked.

"Yeah, he's interested in investing in the movie version of Gladstone's book."

"It's not even a finished story?"

"What difference does that make? You're talking about a business that creates TV content out of shitty Twitter accounts. At least it's got pages and a cover. Besides, he's no dummy. He sees this thing's got legs."

"Oh, yeah, about that," I said, getting out of the car. "I think you need a lawyer. I've seen bookstores selling their own versions of Gladstone's book now. But you own the rights, right?"

"No it's fine. I cut deals."

"What deals?"

We headed to the garage elevator and Margo pushed the button.

"I gave the major chains the right to publish their own editions for a time," she said. "They bore the printing cost, which wasn't too bad considering the book had to maintain its humble appearance. And they had to agree not to sell it for more than a dollar."

"Why so cheap?"

"Because I'm not interested in book sales right now. We're spreading the word. Just like the Gladstone masks. Slim profit margin there too."

"What word?" I asked. "The Messiah Movement's or the movie?"

Margo scanned the buttons inside the elevator, pushing the uppermost floor, and then turned to me. In her heels, we were eye to eye. "If you're going to save the world, Aaron, you better make it profitable. Unlike handguns and cigarettes, justice doesn't have a lobby."

We had to give credentials to a receptionist and then take another elevator to the roof. I could see all of Sydney, including what I immediately considered their version of our Space Needle, although I learned later theirs was almost twice the size.

"Why the hell did he want to meet us on the roof?" I said, but Margo just pointed to the sky.

A black helicopter approached, not too different from the one in the Hollywood-sign video or the descriptions

Romaya's neighbors had given, and I stood in front of Margo as a reflex.

"Thanks for the wind blocking, Aaron," she said, "but Reggie's expecting to see me, so I better stand in front."

The helicopter set down and a sixtysomething bearded man with longish, graying hair poked out his head. It was Reginald Stanton, piloting the helicopter solo, wearing some sort of 1980s *Airwolf* jumpsuit.

"G'day, mates!" he shouted. "Hop aboard!"

"They really say that shit, down here, don't they?" I said to Margo.

"They really do," she said. "There's probably a crocodile riding shotgun in that thing."

I'm not sure if she'd been in a helicopter before, but Margo certainly knew how to sit in one. She strapped in and crossed her legs, completely at home riding with a billionaire in the sky while I held on to my hat and tried to get a read on this man who apparently had everything he wanted. I wondered if he thought he could add Margo to that collection.

"So, Ms. Zmena, who's your plus-one?" he asked once he got his bearings. We were flying to his estate on Manly Beach.

"Mr. Stanton, let me introduce you to Former Special Agent Aaron Rowsdower."

"Fuck me," he said, turning his head to look at me. "From the book?"

"One and the same," Margo said with a two-hand presentation.

"Bloody great," he said, taking a closer look. "But, um, I can't—"

"I've had extensive reconstructive dental surgery," I said, cutting him off.

"Well, that explains it. Sit tight, mates. We'll be home in a moment."

I tried to talk to Stanton about ICANN and the latest Internet blackout, but I didn't get much from him. He was too busy making more turns and dives than you would have thought necessary for a straight shot to Manly. Still, I kept pressing.

"I thought you were a *former* agent," he said at one point. Another time he corrected me when I said cyber-attacks had shut the Net down. "Cyberattacks have made the Net vulnerable and unreliable," he said. "But your president has shut the Net down. He's switched it off at the hubs again."

With all the traveling and spotty Internet, I hadn't followed the news in the last thirty-six hours. I wasn't sure if that was public knowledge or if Stanton had inside information or if it was just his pet theory. But I knew it would be a mistake to push harder without gaining his trust, so I sat back and watched the bluest water I'd ever seen get closer and closer as he brought Margo and me to Manly.

Stanton said he wanted to take us to one of his nearby homes because he hated doing business at the office, and when we landed he was like a new man. No longer the manic pilot, he was now the manic host, telling us where to sit, pointing out the massaging gadgets in all his reclining chairs and playing bartender, all while answering periodic calls from his bar phone and conducting business. This was definitely a man who cut million-dollar deals while taking a shit.

"First off," Stanton said as we settled into his leopard-skin recliners that overlooked the ocean through a huge plate-glass window, "I love, love, love that Internet Apocalypse book! Really speaks to what's going on in the world right now."

"I think so," Margo said, taking a sip of Stanton's creation, a drink he called a "Koala Fucker." He'd poured one for each of us even though I'd requested a Johnnie Walker on the rocks. I was figuring this guy had blue label.

"I really think you're onto something, and I want on board," he said. "But before we reach out to production companies and studios, I wanted to know if you've thought about making changes."

"Well, of course, in bringing something to the screen there's always going to be liberties you take to convey the story, coupled with the fact that Gladstone's life and this Internet Apocalypse story is still a work in progress."

"Totally," Stanton said, and took two big pulls of Koala Fucker through a Krazy Straw. "I was thinking, what if we told Gladstone's story via a bunch of twentysomethings in San Francisco?"

"I can see the demographic appeal of that," Margo said with the poker face of a champ, "but I think it's important to all those people who are buying the book to see Gladstone's story. That's why I bought the rights. That's the story I want to tell."

"Well, OK," Stanton said. "But Gladstone's such a sook. Like, have a cry, mate. We get it. You gonna follow a bloke like that around?" He sat on a high stool behind his bar and looked down at us.

"Well," Margo began, "I don't really see him like that. . . ."

"OK, well, you've met him," Stanton said. "You tell me. What's your mate about?"

"That's not easy to put simply. I mean, you read his book, but I can tell you from meeting him, Gladstone believes in pure things."

"I don't know what that means," Stanton said, and Margo went into her pitch about the father at the dollar store.

"Oh, for fuck's sake," Stanton interrupted. "I've heard that one already, love."

"Burke?" she asked.

"Yeah, your next president is spewing that one all over his town hall meetings while blaming Obama for corrupting the Net. If that's the best ya got on Gladstone, I'm still leaning toward San Franciscan twentysomethings."

The phone rang, freeing Margo from maintaining her frozen smile. It wasn't good news. "When?" Stanton barked into the phone. "How?" He kept asking questions as he slammed things around behind the bar. Cursing. "I'll be there Wednesday. No, not Tuesday. I'm in Australia. It's already Tuesday here. I own an airline, not a time machine, you fuckwit. Jesus fucking Christ."

"What's wrong?" I asked, but all his anger didn't end with the call. He moved behind the bar like he was trapped in his own home, sweeping shattered glass into a garbage can with his bare hands and shooting furtive glances at Margo and me. Mostly me.

"My friend Michiko was just murdered," he said, and stepped out from behind the bar, wiping his hands together to flick the shards of glass away like dust.

"I'm sorry," Margo said.

"Thank you," he said. "So I'm afraid I'm going to have cut our discussion short. ICANN's called for an emergency conference in California to address."

"Was your friend part of ICANN?" I asked.

"She was a crypto officer," Margo explained on Stanton's behalf. I'm guessing Margo had a manila folder of clippings about her somewhere too.

"Michiko Nagasoto was more than just a crypto officer," Stanton said. "Michiko was brilliant. A programmer, a businesswoman. And beautiful. The point is, she's carked it. Fucking shot dead in Tokyo. Right through her apartment window."

I straightened up my recliner and put my cocktail glass down on the table to my side. Partly because I felt like I was on a case again, and partly because Stanton was making me nervous as he got closer. Something wasn't right.

"Are there any leads?" I asked as he kept pacing.

"Leads? What kind of leads do you mean, Former Special Agent Rowsdower?"

I looked at Margo, who shared my confusion, but I could tell from the way her eyes stayed fixed over my shoulder that Stanton had stopped pacing. He was behind me.

"Y'know, clues?" I asked, turning in my chair, but Stanton rushed up behind me and wrapped his left arm around my neck before I got all the way around. I just barely caught a glimpse of him lifting what looked like a nine-inch blade over his head.

"Are you in danger, Margo?" Stanton asked, but before she had a chance to answer, I grabbed my glass off the table and threw it back over my head and into his face. I heard the thud of what I imagined was Stanton's forehead, and in the moment he flinched I reached back to grab a fistful of his hair with my left hand, pulling him forward over my right shoulder as I stood. He wasn't a small man, but I tend to have extra resolve when someone's trying to murder me. I kept pulling more of his torso over my shoulder, until I had enough leverage to throw the rest of him over and away. His feet hit the high-top stools at the bar before he landed on his back. Somehow he kept hold of the knife, and I stepped on his wrist before he had a chance to use it. That's when the fucker started biting. He rolled to his right and latched on to my right leg, sinking his teeth in hard.

"Goddammit!" I screamed, kicking him in the head with my left foot. "Get off my leg you fucking . . . dingo!"

Margo rushed to the floor and managed to pry the knife from his hands.

"Stop biting me," I said. "I don't want to hurt you."

Stanton finally relented when Margo was standing over him with the knife, and I took my foot off his wrist. "What the fuck was that about?"

"Sorry," he said, getting to his feet and holding his fingers to the blood dripping from where my glass hit his head. "Something's not right, and you're a stranger in my home."

"I'm here because you flew me here, you biting asshole."

He laughed. "Good on ya, mate. I deserved that."

"You're not getting this. If I had my gun, you'd be dead now. You strangled and pulled a knife on your guest, not an intruder. I would have been in my rights. Even in Australia I assume."

"I'm sorry. You're right. I'm not used to things being taken from me. Michiko was more than just my friend."

He sat down on the floor and pushed his hands through his hair, streaking blood across the gray. He couldn't be bothered applying pressure. He just sat for a moment with his head down. Occassionally, blood dripped on his fingers tightly gripped in front of him in a vengeful prayer. Margo sat down next to him and put her hand on his shoulder but did not speak. After another minute, I sat down too, directly across from him.

"Reginald," I said. "Please look at me."

He lifted his head. "She was such a light sleeper," he said. "Not like me. Every morning, I'd wake, and if she were even there at all she'd be dressed, or working out something on her laptop. I missed so many waking hours of her life while I snored away like a mad cunt. But a couple of times, not often, but a couple of times, I woke for some stupid reason, and she'd be sleeping. I'd lie as still as I could so I could watch her, but she'd always wake up seconds later. But in those few moments she was so peaceful. So . . . small."

He lost it again, and Margo moved her hand to the back of his neck.

"Not that we were going to get married," he said. "People like us aren't built for that. She had some wog in France, and I'm always off banging models like a . . ."

"Mad cunt?" Margo offered.

"Something like that," Stanton said. "But I always thought I'd have a morning where I'd wake first. Just one morning for me to tell her I'd watched her sleep, small and beautiful, for hours."

I gave Stanton my handkerchief and he pressed it to his forehead.

"Sorry about the biting, mate," he said.

"And the attempted murder?" I asked.

"Yeah, it's been a hard day."

"I know you heard the story about the dollar store," I said. "Even if it was from Hamilton Burke's lips, but let me tell you something else about Gladstone. Something that might be hard for you to understand with all your homes, money, and power. Your loss today—even though it's awful and I'm sorry—only scratches the surface of his. Gladstone lost his wife. First in divorce and then again when she was murdered right in front of him. He lost his job, which believe me, does something to you. For a while Gladstone lost his mind, and when he got it back he lost his freedom, detained for crimes he did not commit under the bullshit NET Recovery Act. Now he's lost his country, and he's on the run and hiding somewhere, and I can't find him."

"So he's a loser? Is that the point?"

"Oh man, you're a prick," I said. "No, the point is, if you took that many things away from most men, there'd be nothing left. What are you, Reggie, without your airline, stores, and companies? What are you without the people you love? Gladstone lost everything, and there was still too much of a person left over for the remains to be blown away in the wind. He didn't put a bullet in his brain. He didn't pull a knife on anyone else. He told people that pure things still existed. That they mattered and people mattered. And he may have done it like some rambling, drunken asshole, but now there are people all over the world holding up signs, spraying logos, and they're doing it because they believe it's possible that if you stick it out long enough, everything that's been destroyed can be returned."

By this point, I realized I was standing and ready to go. Even if I didn't know where I was going. Even if Margo was crying. Reginald stood too.

"I believe the people who killed your friend, killed his wife," I said. "I believe this all has something to do with the Internet, and I'm going to keep looking for Gladstone until I figure out where he is. And then I'm going to help him, because it feels like work, and work makes me feel like who I'm supposed to be, and that's all I know. That's everything I know."

"That was beautiful, mate," Stanton said. Then he turned to Margo. "See? There's your leading man."

Report 8

Stanton was good enough to fly us back to Sydney before he went off to California. I thought about following him out there, but Margo wasn't ready to leave.

"We're in another Apocalypse," I said. "A member of ICANN has been murdered, and they're holding a meeting right now."

"I understand that," she replied. "Let them have their meetings. You won't learn anything more until they happen. Besides, you deserve a vacation."

Margo clearly didn't know how lazy I'd been the preceding month, but I agreed to stay back a few days and reconnect after the ICANN meetings. Stanton gave us the number of his L.A. landline so we could reach him.

We had dinner that night at some fusion place Margo was excited to try. She and the server had a long talk about tomatoes. Afterward we got rooms at a hotel for one night, and agreed we'd figure out longer-term plans in the morning. That night, I heard the phone ring in Margo's room. I did a good job of not listening. I didn't want to hear her speaking to her boyfriend. So I distracted myself, reading the pamphlets in my room about local attractions, and when that wasn't enough, I grinded my leg into a bag of ice on the bed, rubbing the cubes where a batshit Australian billionaire had devoured my calf only hours before.

The next morning, Margo was in good spirits and had decided we should be proper tourists. "Let's take the ferry to Manly," she said.

"What's there besides Stanton's place?" I asked.

"Who cares?" she said. "We're gonna take the ferry back once we get there anyway, but it passes right by the Sydney Opera House."

I'm not sure if there's much diversity in ferry design but the boat we got on looked just like the one in New York that takes you to Staten Island. Or, at least that's my memory. I hadn't taken it in years, and I certainly didn't try to accost Gladstone on it the way he imagined in his journal. The only difference I could see between the Staten Island Ferry and this one was Aussies had no problem leaving tripping hazards around because, I guess, no one sues here. I stumbled over some rope left on the deck, catching myself on the railing.

"You all right?" Margo asked.

"Fine," I said, even though the bite marks in my calf were flaring up.

Margo was happy, and why not? This Australian "winter" felt to be a lovely seventy degrees and the sky and water were having a fuck-you contest to see who could be more blue. I'd seen a bubbling giddiness in Margo that made her move in tiny hops when she let it, but today she was also keeping watch, not completely at ease.

"Grab us a seat on the left side," she said. "Opera House side. I have to find a bathroom."

I sat on a bench along the outside of the ferry and tried to pretend I was on vacation. After all, this was how I'd probably dress if I ever took one. I was wearing some comfortable brown shoes, jeans, a button-down shirt, and a sports jacket. Maybe I'd lose the sports jacket, but it made me feel more like me. I wasn't ready for Hawaiian shirts yet.

The Harbour Bridge reminded me of New York too, but it was different, and not just because it was newer than anything back home. I knew it connected the business district with North Sydney, but it didn't look like something to use for business commuting. Maybe it was the sun, graciously shielded by Gladstone's hat, but it glimmered in a blue sky like some sort of leisure bridge, only to be traveled for a good time. Maybe it was because I could see where the bridge came from and where it was going and both places looked shiny. I wasn't sure, but that's when I realized Margo had made a mistake. If I was staring at the bridge, then the Opera House had to be on the other side.

I considered waiting, but I figured Margo would appreciate it if I got us a seat on the right side before the boat filled up. Besides, she was no frail thing. If she came back from the bathroom, finding me gone, I knew it would only take her a moment to realize what was going on, so I worked my way to the right side of the ship, this time keeping watch for tripping hazards. I was pleased when I caught sight of the Opera House. After the last few weeks, it felt good to be right about something, although my concerns about seats filling up were unwarranted. Commuter rush was over and the ferry was nearly empty. I was also wrong about something else. Margo was already on this side, unless there was another five-ten woman in Australia wearing the same thin, black buttoned sweater thing and jeans. I knew it was Margo even with her back to me.

She was talking to someone, but I couldn't see his face. Just a stylish fedora peeking out over the top of Margo's short dirty-blond hair. For a second, I wondered if she'd mistaken him for me because of the hat, but that was stupid. Even as I got closer, I couldn't make out his face. He seemed to be hiding behind a newspaper with a banner headline reading, HERE WE GO AGAIN! There was a picture of a computer with one of those circle-slashes through it, which maybe wasn't the best way to convey a government shutdown of the Internet at the hubs, but that's a tough thing to convey visually. Also, journalism wasn't my main concern. I wanted to know why Margo put me on the wrong side of the ferry while she talked to this prick behind a paper.

I kept walking and didn't stop until I was standing in front of them both. He couldn't see me, but Margo could.

"Aaron," she said, looking more surprised than when I showed up unannounced outside her boyfriend's place.

The paper came down slowly, and there beneath the stylish fedora was a face I knew very well, at least the eyes. The rest was somehow different. Leaner and more angular than the face from my memories.

"Gladstone?" I asked.

The engines kicked in and the ferry started to move. He threw his paper and broke toward the back of the boat. Margo grabbed him by the arm.

"I told you. He's all right!" she said.

It was Gladstone. I could see by the way he ran, and I rushed to put myself in his way. "Besides," I said. "This ferry's in motion, so unless you've got an inflatable raft, I think you're stuck with me."

He glared back at Margo. I'd seen that look from many failed conspiracies. The accused staring down an informant in court.

"I was trying to tell you," Margo said, "but some jackass showed up sooner than he was supposed to." The last part was directed to me.

Gladstone stood up straight and stared at me, and I realized it wasn't just his face that was leaner. He was in better shape than I'd ever seen him.

I took off the fedora I'd been keeping safe for him these many months. "Gladstone," I said, holding the hat out, "I think that fedora's maybe a touch too fancy for your T-shirt and flannel. I think I have a better one for you."

"My hat?" he said, taking it from me.

"Yes," I said. "I found it at LAX. Had it cleaned best I could."

Gladstone sat down with the hat in his lap, running

two fingers slowly across the crease at the top. I sat down next to him.

"Thank you, Aaron," he said, "but you keep it. I mean, what kind of douchebag owns more than one fedora?"

He handed it back to me, almost relieved not to claim it.

"Where'd you get that new one?" I asked.

Gladstone seemed confused, and I turned to Margo, but she shared his expression.

The Opera House was in my peripheral vision and I turned to see its peaks and pitched egg spires up close. From pictures, I always thought the Opera House was a bunch of echo chambers designed for acoustics, but where I expected an opening, there was glass, designed to reveal what was being kept from you. I turned back around to Gladstone and Margo, and they no longer seemed confused. Now they were just a couple.

"*You're* Parker?" I asked.

Gladstone nodded with urgent, open eyes, dictating discretion even though the next person near us was a good twelve feet away.

"I thought you'd realize that as soon as you saw him," Margo said. "Or sooner actually . . ."

And now I felt like the fingered con. "Oh, I realized one thing," I said to Margo. "I knew you weren't telling me everything, didn't I?"

"Don't blame her," Gladstone said. "I asked Margo to keep my secret. She always trusted you. I didn't."

"Oh, that's right," I said. "I'm that asshole from your stupid book. And by the way . . ." I pulled back my lips with two fingers on each side, sticking my clenched teeth in Gladstone's face. "Take a look. What's the problem?"

Gladstone laughed hard, his whole body shaking the silkscreen of Ziggy Stardust's face on his shirt.

"Do you know how much shit I've taken because of you?" I asked.

"I'm sorry, Aaron," he said. "I already apologized for that back in L.A. And the trust thing's not personal. I have to be careful who I let in. Things have gone badly. . . ."

I turned back to the water. The Opera House was long in the distance, and all I could see was water and the skyline. Everything looked bright and clean in this country that seemed specially designed for second chances.

"I'm sorry about Romaya," I said. "I know you had nothing to do with that."

"Thank you," he said.

Manly was coming into view, and I didn't want to create another pressure that sent Gladstone running.

"First of all," Margo said. "I want to apologize to both of you." She stood up for added formality. "Aaron, I'm sorry I didn't tell you sooner that I knew where Gladstone was, but it wasn't my secret to tell. A person has a right not to be found."

"Yeah, that's what I thought," Gladstone said.

"I know you did, Parker, and I'm sorry. I'm sorry I tricked you into meeting Rowsdower. But I had to get you out of, y'know, Gladstone."

That's when I realized what I was seeing on Margo's face that day she left his place. Gladstone was supposed to go with her to Sydney. But they must have fought when he refused to leave.

Gladstone didn't speak and he wasn't looking at Margo, but I also knew he was listening. It seemed not listening to her would never occur to him.

"You've carved out a safe space, and I'm glad," she said. "You deserve it. You're in control of your life, living there and deciding what comes in and what stays out. I'm lucky you chose to let me in. . . ."

"But?" he asked.

"But . . . you've done enough mining there. It's time to go."

"That should have been my decision," he said.

"Sometimes people need help doing the right thing," I offered, but Gladstone just eyed the approaching dock.

"But I will say, in my defense," Margo added, "I'm not sorry the two of you are together. This is right."

It sounded like words a CEO would say, and rang in my ears like business-speak, but anyone looking at Margo could see her joy, and any cop could see what she was feeling: the relief that comes from ending lies. A relief felt only by people who value the truth. That's when I realized I was the only one there with a secret, because I never told Margo how I felt, and now there was no point in doing so.

"We'll be docking in a moment," she said, "and I'm going to leave, but what I would like is for you boys to grab another ticket and ride back to Sydney."

"Without you?" Gladstone asked.

"Yes, and then buy another in Sydney and come back to find me. You'll need the time alone together. You need to figure out how you fit."

When we pulled into the dock, Margo left ahead of us, keeping her departure brief and professional with a very tiny and platonic wave, equally distributed to Gladstone and me. I was glad I didn't have to see a goodbye kiss, and as I watched her walk away I realized that restraint was a deliberate kindness for my benefit. There were no secrets anymore.

"Y'know, Gladstone," I said, "you still dress like such a fucking asshole." He laughed. "I mean, Bowie's fedora, a Bowie T-shirt, jeans, and a flannel?"

"Don't forget the Doc Martens," he said. "Gen X rules."

Gladstone didn't run when we got to the Manly terminal, but he didn't speak either. And when he pulled a wallet from his jeans, I saw the muscles in his forearm flex. I assumed his improved build was the result of his new-found mining occupation, but I couldn't help feeling there was more to it than a more active vocation. It was like magic, especially because he seemed to have lost the ten pounds I'd gained. Now aside from the five-inch difference in our height and his atrocious fashion sense, we were more alike than ever.

We sat side by side on the way back, drinking our coffees instead of speaking. I thought it was important to let him initiate the conversation. To let him know he wasn't my prisoner. Finally, he said, "It was kind of you to keep my hat. Thank you."

"Well, y'know, it's evidence," I said.

"Unwanted evidence you got from a lost and found, and had cleaned?" he replied.

There was no use arguing. "You're welcome."

"Can I call you, Rowsdower now?" he asked. "Y'know, without the 'Special Agent'?"

"Even better, you could call me Aaron."

"Well, where's the fun in that?" he asked, and repeated "Rowsdower" two more times, getting the most out of each syllable. "Rowsdower, Rowsdower." Then he stopped. "Sorry, Aaron, but could you take off the hat for a second?"

Gladstone removed his, and I obliged when he turned to face me. We were closer without the brims in the way, and he stared at me for a very long time. It wasn't invasive, because with that kind of proximity, he was revealing himself as much as he inspected. Finally, he whispered, "Hamilton Burke murdered Romaya."

I'd heard Gladstone say insane things before. I'd seen him at his worst—drunk and delusional. But this time he was only haunted. Still looking for monsters, but from a safe and sober place. Only the content of his speech was unhinged.

"How do you know?"

Gladstone didn't blink or take offense. "Hamilton Burke blew up the Hollywood sign." He was slightly louder.

"Why would—"

"Hamilton Burke blew up that trolley at the Farmers Market."

"Wait, you're saying that—"

"Hamilton Burke is the one who first shut down the Internet."

"Wait, wait, wait," I said, standing up. "You know all of this for a fact?" I stared down at Gladstone, who was still as calm and immovable as the Bowie fedora sitting on his lap.

"Why were you looking for me, Aaron?"

"Because I had a hunch," I said, retaking my seat.

"Yes?"

"That you'd seen something awful. That it had driven

you away. And that it was also all tied up with the Internet somehow."

He twitched with incredulity. "Yeah, well, you were right. About all of it. Good for you. So what are *you* running from?"

"I'm not running from anything. I'm evaluating the evidence. What's this based on? Not a confession, because Burke certainly didn't reveal his plans when you met him in New York—unless you left that part out of your journal."

"No, he didn't, but I met him again at the Playboy mansion in L.A."

I made a face.

"It happened," he insisted.

"A confession?"

"Well, no, it was more like he was bragging, and it wasn't at the mansion . . ."

Gladstone had lost his momentum, and I was getting annoyed, but he wasn't lying. He was stalling. He was ashamed.

"Hamilton penetrated Anonymous," he said.

"What does that mean?"

"Remember Quiffmonster42 from the book? That was Hamilton the whole time."

"What are you talking about? Anonymous got Tobey and Jeeves out of jail. They hacked the security footage I told them about. Fuck, they helped you too. You're on that film clearly not blowing up the sign."

"I know that, and that's Burke's helicopter. The same one he used to kill Romaya. I'm not saying he's *all* of Anonymous. He penetrated it, but Anonymous is not one man or one thing, and it's hard to tell the good because,

y'know"—Gladstone waved his hand in front of his
face—"they wear masks!"

Gladstone got up to defuse some of his energy, and I
thought again about what Professor Leonards had said
about miracles and disasters.

"He had my confidence the entire time I was in L.A.
He was popping up, getting information, putting me on
missions."

"Oh, really," I said. "I can't imagine what that must
have been like for you."

Gladstone stopped pacing for a moment. "My letters?"
he asked.

"Yeah, your letters. Mind telling me what you had me
doing? Running around to ICANN key holders like your
errand boy?"

"First of all, you weren't my errand boy, and I'm getting to all that."

"Well, maybe you could reach your point before we
hit Sydney. Why would Hamilton Burke be after a guy
like you? You tweet something about his mom?"

"I don't remember you being this funny," Gladstone
said. "Anyway, it wasn't personal. It was business. I was
in his way and I'd gotten too big to kill."

Gladstone could see I didn't believe him. He was a
Gen-X kid who had spent the last several years basking
online in a Millennial mentality. Pushing forty and still
somehow thinking he was special.

"I know I'm not important, Aaron," he said. "But it
was the book. You saw. It got big. I was getting a following. If he killed me, I'd be a martyr and then I'd really be
a messiah."

Gladstone sat back down, knowing I'd make him go

through it all again. I felt bad because I knew telling things to another person, face-to-face, makes them real, but I'd labored long enough without all the facts.

"He played me. When I was locked up at the Veterans' Affairs Building, he was busy discrediting both me and Anonymous. The bombings at that movie theater and the Farmers Market that happened near the Messiah Movement symbols? That was just the start of him muddying the waters. He led me to that Hollywood sign and blew it up too. He wanted my friends arrested. He wanted to make me look like a terrorist. But that wasn't enough. It wasn't even enough to kill Romaya. He framed me for that too."

If any man were powerful enough to effect that level of corruption, I knew it would be a billionaire, so that was the means, but I still had no motive for Burke to do any of these things.

"He got me my passport and my last three thousand dollars and put both in my hands while I was still wet with her blood," Gladstone said, and now he was shaking. A quiver in his voice, his lower lip. "He even drove me to the fucking airport."

"To shroud you in disgrace? To drive you to suicide?"

"Ya think?" Gladstone barked.

"I believe you, Gladstone, but I'm not seeing a lot of motive here. And now, because of Anonymous, you've been cleared of the Hollywood-sign bombing, and frankly it seems law enforcement would rather forget that homicide ever happened than pin it on you."

"I don't want them to forget about it. I want Burke to pay."

"Then what are you doing hiding in Australia? Playing house with Margo? I don't see Burke paying. I see him running for president."

I decided to stand up. After all, I could see Fort Denison coming up in the distance. I recognized it from the hotel pamphlets the night before. Locals called it Pinchgut Island because the prisoners were marooned there with limited rations. Soon this ride would be over and once we got off this boat I might have to start all over again.

Gladstone got up too. "Do you know why you never found me, Aaron?" he asked.

"I did find you," I said.

"Yes, eventually. But even after reading the love letters and spending all that time with Margo, you were still surprised to find me with her."

I could make out the fort more clearly, its circular stone base rising into a squat tower.

"You were looking for a broken man," he continued. "But I'm not broken. I work now. I'm loved. And I am planning."

"That's great, Gladstone," I said. "Except I did find you. I'm here. And what's more, if you're not still broken, then why are you hiding on the other side of the world? You're even working in a mine for chrissakes."

Gladstone laughed. "You think it's like a cave, with a flashlight and pickaxe? It's the twenty-first century. I drive a truck and move minerals around. I'm outdoors and everything."

"You know what I mean," I said.

"Yeah, I do, but go fuck yourself because I'm not hiding, I'm becoming more than me. I'm becoming an idea.

You see the signs? The slogans, the masks? I'm making myself something too big for Hamilton to kill."

"No, I don't see that. I see Margo promoting a movie. Are you growing a movement or a brand? You're not planning from your castle. You're in exile. You might as well hop on another raft and paddle away to this penal colony."

"Wow, you've become such a poet since I've seen you. Two more years out of work, maybe you'll be me."

"I'm already you. Doing your job and running around wherever you tell me. How much longer can you stay here?"

"I'm not leaving until I can destroy him."

"And when's that?"

"I don't know."

"You don't know or you won't tell me?"

"I don't know."

"Why not?"

"Because I don't understand what he's doing with the Net. I sincerely believe he took it away because he could. What he told me in New York seemed sincere. He was fucking with it, almost magnanimously."

"That stuff he said about technology only increasing the expectation of productivity?"

"Right, but then I think he saw an angle. A way to return it for profit, and I don't know the details, but the government became complicit at some point. They had to. It's too big for one man to take down, and he knew it would come back in a new form."

"And it has. "

"Right. And the government's shut it down again, but he's also running for president, railing against them, so I don't have it all worked out."

We were pulling into Sydney. I could hear the few tourists on board heading to the front of the ferry. "You don't have to have it all worked out. You have actual crimes to hit him with. Murder, terrorism, we'll worry about nailing him for the conspiracy later."

"Who would believe me? I fled. I'm living in Australia under an assumed identity."

"Yeah, how'd you manage that anyway?"

"It's all Margo. She has connections from her old job like you wouldn't believe. All Hollywood shit. Y'know during the Cuban embargo, all the biggest Hollywood actors had their own private humidor locker of cigars on Cuba. They'd just land their private jets and pick up their stash."

"I'll make a note of that, thank you. Very helpful, Gladstone."

"Anyway, I'm a fugitive and he's fucking Hamilton Burke. No one will believe me."

"I believe you," I said. Then I did something I'd only done once before, and that was when I was putting Gladstone in handcuffs: I touched him. I laid my hand on his shoulder and added, "I know how to build a case. Burke didn't pull the trigger, fly the helicopter, and plant the bombs himself, did he?"

"No," Gladstone replied.

"Right. So he had help, and help always leaves loose ends. There's always someone who will talk. So who are his collaborators?"

"I don't know," Gladstone said. "I'm not in his head."

"Yeah, well, I know someone who could be, and he's not in jail anymore."

"Jeeves?"

I smiled and so did Gladstone.

"Son," I said, "grab your things, I've come to take you home."

My plan of attack required Gladstone, Margo, and me to check in with Jeeves in New York and Stanton in California, but Stanton had promised us a week of ICANN meetings, and there was no sense in trying to deal with the Apocalypse until all the information was in, so we headed to New York first. Gladstone had kept Jeeves's landline, and I placed the call, making sure everyone's favorite psychic was back home before we departed. I didn't mention Gladstone. No form of communication could be trusted.

While Gladstone's alias, Parker Lawrence, wasn't real, his passport containing that name and his picture certainly was—issued by the Australian government. He'd make it past customs if the government were even looking for him, which from Dunican's last press conference didn't seem to be the case. But that only calmed Gladstone so much. I saw him checking blind corners for danger. I'd seen him do that before, but now his furtive glances weren't accompanied by wild gesticulations. His agitation went inside instead of out.

We had a two-hour layover at LAX before we could get to New York, and we were all tired and hungry from the flight.

"I gotta get a burger in me or maybe some fish and chips," Gladstone said.

We settled up at a different faceless bar and grill, the three of us taking a table for four. Gladstone and I hung our fedoras off the back of the empty chair. When the waitress came, Margo ordered a vodka and soda, and, I, weaning off my drunken month, got a beer. Gladstone ordered a Diet Coke.

"That's new," I said.

"I haven't had a drink in months," he replied.

"Found religion?" I asked.

"It's not that," he replied. "I'm just waiting for the right occasion."

I looked to Margo. "He won't tell me," she said. "I thought getting Bowie's fedora would qualify, but apparently not."

"Anyway," Gladstone said, "how are we going to get Jeeves and Burke in touching distance?"

"I would think anyone who made a big enough contribution to his campaign would get a handshake," Margo offered.

"Yeah, except he's not taking contributions," I said. "Burke's self-funding his campaign so he's not beholden to special interests."

"Which would be great, except now he's completely beholden to his own interests," Gladstone added.

"Just a second," Margo said. "I'm sorry I have to ask this, but I've never met Jeeves. Are you both really saying he can do this? Take a hand and read a mind?"

Gladstone and I spoke in unison and without hesitation: "Yes."

I went over the plan again. "First, Jeeves gets us the names. Any collaborator, any bank account, any information he can."

"I know you're focusing on the crimes," Gladstone interrupted, "but I'm still hoping Jeeves can tell us Burke's endgame with the Internet too. I just wish I knew what he wanted."

"We will. But first bombs and bullets. We get his collaborators. Then we feed that information to my man at Anonymous, and—"

"Whom you trust?" Gladstone asked.

"What do you want me to tell you, Gladstone? He's one for one. He already got Jeeves and Tobey out of jail," I said, dropping down to a whisper. "I'd say have him pass a Jeeves test, but I don't think it makes sense to risk Jeeves on that. Jeeves is our ace in the hole for Burke."

Gladstone nodded in agreement and took a notepad from his corduroy sports jacket.

"What are you doing," I asked. "Taking notes or something?"

Gladstone looked surprised. "Well, no. I mean, if we're really doing this," he said, "I thought I'd go back to writing it all down like I did before."

"Uh, that's not necessary," I said, pulling my folder of typed reports from the carry-on at my feet.

"Well, that's great, Aaron," he said, "but, y'know, I mean, my book *did* go paper viral. . . ."

"Look, let's not bicker," Margo said. "As executive producer, I'm going to retain the power to make any story changes anyway, so we can worry about your battling manuscripts later."

Gladstone kept his notebook open, and I flipped my reports over so I'd have a blank sheet in front of me even though I typically typed my reports up at the end of the day.

"Besides, I have a more important concern," Margo

said. "How effective is Anonymous even going to be if the Net is still down?"

That was a good point. The latest news reports were that the Net would creep back to life, one site at a time, as the government verified traffic, security protocols, and "vulnerability." It was a full-scale audit to keep out the one bad apple that would spoil the bunch.

"Well, Anonymous is more than the Internet. They can hack closed systems too. As long as they can communicate, hopefully they can find the right people, but we have no choice. We put the Jeeves part of the plan in motion, and have faith that enough of the Net will be there for Anonymous."

"Now who's found religion?" Gladstone asked.

"Well, if we don't have faith, we better have patience," I said.

Gladstone put his notebook away. "Sometimes they're the same thing."

Since our plans were up in the air, we decided to crash at my place the first night back. I had to believe the two of them, who had been very arm's-length and professional in my presence, wouldn't make me endure a night of passion through the wall. They were fine with the idea as well. We all just wanted to shower and sleep after a long flight, even though it was still early evening by the time we got to my place. Also, with communications being impaired somewhat as they were, we wanted to stay together until we saw Jeeves.

We took a car service home from JFK, but only after I insisted upon paying for it.

"Fine," Margo said, "but I just made you a producer, so be sure to deduct it from your taxes."

As the car pulled up to my apartment, I saw a silver Chevy Tahoe double-parked outside.

"Keep going," I told the driver. "Take a right at the corner and drop me at Northern Boulevard."

"You said, 210–50, Forty-first Ave.?" he replied.

"Just do it, please. It's one more block."

"What's going on?" Gladstone asked.

"There's a government car parked outside my apartment," I said. "I'll see what it is, but when I get out, you keep going. Meet with Jeeves. Do what we said and do not contact me. I will find you. Maybe it's nothing, but I'm not taking chances."

Margo put her hand on Gladstone's knee, and he covered it, slowly working his fingers between hers before wrapping them around into her palm. He took a deep breath. I unzipped my briefcase and handed him the folder containing all my reports and said, "Don't fuck it up. I'll see you soon."

Day 424

For the last six months, I haven't written anything except letters to Margo, and that's been enough. I give her all the thoughts and feelings that used to bang around inside and drive me. But it hasn't been a deluge, no floodgate of emotions spilling on the floor. Instead, I struggle to explain, searching for a level of specificity no normal person would care about. And she can't be normal either, because she listens and helps me refine, in the shared belief that everything must be tied to the right words before it can be released. And when that happens we sit and stare at it outside of ourselves. We categorize it and put it on a brightly lit shelf, where it can never surprise or control us again. And I say "us" because I think I do this for her as well. That is what we can do for each other.

It creates space inside me. It gives me room to accept more. To let more in. And although I pulled my notebook in that airport bar, I have to believe it was a reflex, because riding into the city with Margo, it was hard to imagine what I'd be writing for.

"For Aaron," Margo said. "He'll want notes."

Apparently, I was talking out loud. I did that with Margo sometimes too. Usually by saying "I love you" without even realizing it when I was next to her in a quiet moment.

It was past eight when we got to the Upper West Side and we decided to crash at a hotel. We'd call Jeeves in the morning.

"You think Rowsdower's OK?" I asked, lying next to Margo in a room kept dark by thick pulled curtains.

"I think so. Besides, he's no dope and he's got a good cover now. Even if someone wants to know why he's poking around, he can say he's a producer on the film. Doing some film consulting. Government guys do that all the time."

It was a comforting thought.

"How does it feel to be home, baby?" she asked.

"In the dark, next to you, it feels the same," I said, putting my arm around her waist and pulling her to me. "Ask me again in the morning."

The next day, I left my Bowie fedora and sports jacket back at the room, not only to look less like Gladstone but also because it was incredibly hot. At breakfast, I poked at my eggs at Andrews Coffee Shop and still couldn't answer Margo's question. How did it feel? Everything looked the same for the most part, but I wasn't sure I'd come home. I couldn't imagine having a life like our Dominican waitress, who was good enough to remember that Margo's toast was wheat and mine was white, although she seemed to have a perfectly fine life. The owner, who barked at his staff in Greek from in front of the grill window, also seemed deeply rooted in his surroundings, but his life made little sense to me either. You get up, pay rent, yell at people to serve food faster. Across the aisle there was a visiting German couple, looking very white and in love. Half their booth was filled with their backpacks, and they ate Belgian waffles and sausages in their shorts and expensive hiking boots. I couldn't see myself tagging along with them either.

Everything seemed to be working really well without me, so what difference did being gone make? Margo was good enough not to pose her question again. She was very good about knowing when I needed more time, but when we walked out in the Midtown early-morning sun, I managed to say, "New York is really big. Just so big." You couldn't see all of this place at once, and being close enough to even a medium-size office building was enough to blot out a skyscraper.

We called Jeeves from a newly refurbished postapocalyptic pay phone so nothing could be traced to the hotel, but got no answer.

"Maybe he's set up shop at Central Park again," I said. "After all, a boy's gotta eat."

So we headed off to Central Park's Bethesda Fountain, where I'd first met Jeeves at the start of the Apocalypse. With so much time passed, I was looking forward to seeing him once again play human search engine for the good people of New York. As we walked north from Columbus

Circle, the park got increasingly crowded. There was a speech or a protest going on. And despite the August heat, there were people dressed like the Gladstone from my journal. Lots of hats and sports jackets, and others were even wearing the Gladstone masks.

There may have been people dressed as Oz, Tobey, and Jeeves too, but you could see people like that in the park on any day. Some college kid in khaki shorts and flip-flops handed me a flier for the Working Party.

"Burke's here," I said. Rage Against the Machine's "Take the Power Back" was coming from the Naumburg Bandshell, a place I'd walked past many times but had rarely seen filled. Its white rounded back reminded me a bit of the Sydney Opera House, but older and more exposed. It was a workday, so the crowd was pretty young, but the place was filled. We worked ourselves through dozens of Gladstones, and it occurred to me I could have stayed hidden better if I'd dressed as myself.

"Look," Margo said, pointing to the banner hanging down from the back of the shell. "I'm gonna fucking sue him."

The banner carried a print of the fedora-wearing Wi-Fi symbol, along with the words THE INTERNET IS PEOPLE AND WE'RE STILL HERE.

"OK," I said. "After we get the murder, terrorism, and global-conspiracy charges to stick, we'll work on your copyright-infringement suit."

Ordinarily Margo would have laughed, but she was too busy waiting for Burke to come out and watching for what it would do to me. He emerged wearing a suit, but not the vest and tie I'd seen before. Also, his hair wasn't slicked back. Margo tried to hold my hand, but I couldn't release my fist.

"Hello, Central Park!" he shouted to the crowd, and the audience reflected his enthusiasm.

The music died down, but no one took their seats. This was like a concert where only old people sat.

"Welcome to Internet Apocalypse 3.0!" he said, and the place went wild. "I've talked about a lot of things on this campaign trail, but today I want to talk to you about the Internet. Because once again, this administration shows us there is nothing they can return, they can't take away."

More cheers.

"The Internet was gone. Then it was back. Then it was gone. Then it was back with a fee. Then it was gone again. And now . . . now is the worst part, my friends. Now the government brings the Internet back on its own terms."

Burke had them completely. Boos emanated from the crowd, and I tightened with hate. I was shaking, and Margo stood so close by my side that I could feel her body move with breathing, and that was good. That was the level of contact I could bear in the moment.

"You watch. This government audit? This investigation into the vulnerability of each and every site to meet government approval? All that is, is government control of the Internet. They'll decide what sites to bring back. They'll decide how fast they'll load. They will control your access to communication and information. It is unacceptable. As your president, I will keep you safe, and I will keep our infrastructure safe, but I will not use it as an excuse to be a technological tyrant."

The place erupted with anger and passion. "Burke! Burke! Burke!"

"But it won't work," he continued. "Not just because it's wrong. And not just because we won't allow it. But because . . . *The Internet Is People . . . and WE'RE. STILL. HERE!*"

And that's when the destruction came, because there was nowhere else to put all the emotion. The crowd started stomping and ripping apart the unused folding chairs.

"Oh my God," Margo said.

"Yeah," I replied.

"No," she continued, "not all this craziness. I mean, I know what Burke wants now."

"Yeah?" I asked.

"Baby, he wants to be you."

"Me?"

"Hamilton Burke wants to be the Internet Messiah."

It was hard to deny Margo's theory in the face of all the rhetoric and branding.

"And if that's the case," Margo added. "It will be very easy to get Jeeves to him."

If Margo had been looking at the bandshell instead of me she would have realized that last part wasn't necessary, because I could see Jeeves already onstage waiting for his introduction.

"Friends, friends," Burke said, raising his hand and regaining their attention, "there's someone I want to bring out. Someone who is well known to Central Park. His name is Dan McCall, but you might know him as Jeeves!"

Jeeves emerged fully from behind the curtain, casually dressed, as always, in shorts and sandals. It seems the Burke campaign had managed to replace his ever-present T-shirt with a nice blue button-down number.

"Hello," he said, and the crowd, filled with park locals, gave him warm applause.

"Y'know, a little over a year ago, I sat not far from here and met the man I thought would return the Internet. The man I proclaimed to be the Internet Messiah."

A few people cheered, especially the guys dressed as but most tempered their enthusiasm to see what e next.

hat man was Gladstone, whom so many of you now from his journal."

re were cheers from people who'd never met ple who'd created a hero out of the man in my

et Gladstone," Jeeves continued. "He's a good I'm relieved at the latest from the NSA that , nor I, nor Brendan Tobey is a suspect in bings. A statement they were only willing to the way, *after* Anonymous released the foot-real perpetrators of that Hollywood-sign de-."

ed for a trace of reaction in Burke's face, but s nothing. He was a stone.

I have a confession. While I still consider Glad-friend, and hope he's safe, wherever he is, walk-water, buying porn, whatever, I think I may have too soon. The point is, while I got the location think the actual man who'll bring back the In-is right next to me. In Hamilton Burke, I see not only Gladstone's belief in a free Internet but also the drive and the ambition to make it happen."

Margo looked at me, but not with sympathy. Maybe she didn't want me to think there was anything about my life to be sorry for, but there was also another possi- bility. Jeeves might have been putting our plan in motion before we ever explained it to him. And why not? Cer- tainly a man as smart as Jeeves was capable of thinking any thought we could. Even more, if Margo were right, and Hamilton really wanted to be me, he might have even sought Jeeves out himself.

"Y'know, back in L.A.," Jeeves said. "Gladstone once told an audience he wasn't the Internet Messiah. Instead the Messiah was all of us. Because any one of us could wear that hat. And so with that in mind, I want to take care of something."

A young female staffer holding a fedora emerged from behind the curtain and handed it off to Jeeves.

"Hamilton Burke," Jeeves said, "I hereby dub you the Internet Messiah!" He placed the fedora on Burke's head like a crown, and the cheers were deafening.

It was too much. No one was looking for me, but I felt I was back in the middle of everything and if something went wrong there was now a frenzied army ready to tear me apart out of love or hate or both. I wanted to leave but I stayed to make sure Jeeves was still my friend. I wanted to see something that would let me leave with all all the fear I was carrying. And then it happened. Right as Burke was straightening his fedora and smiling, Jeeves grabbed his hand and held it over both their heads.

"The Internet Messiah!" he shouted, and raised his other hand too before pumping their embrace in the air.

The crowd grew somehow louder still and that old Carly Simon song came on. Hamilton turned to exit with his music, but Jeeves wouldn't let go. "The Internet Messiah!" he kept screaming, and holding and holding and holding his hand.

Report 9

There was no one in the parked car outside my place, so either the agent was on break or already in my apartment. These guys didn't fuck around. So as I walked back to my apartment from Northern Boulevard, I decided I could do a better job of feigning surprise from a NSA visit if I picked up a few sliders from White Castle along the way.

I could smell Dunican's brand of cigarette, Camel Lights, before I even turned on my lights, but I still did my best to look surprised when I saw him sitting in my dining room.

"Patrick!" I said, dropping my mail to the floor and swallowing the remains of my slider with far too much effort.

"Hello, Aaron," he said. "Hope you don't mind, but y'know, I don't have a toilet in my car and I wasn't sure when you'd be home. It was just easier this way. Plus your locks are bullshit."

"Not at all, Pat," I said. "What's a little breaking and entering between friends?"

He put his cigarette out in my grandmother's candy dish.

"Besides, Pat. I don't really have anything anyone would want to steal. Y'know, government salary and all. . . ."

"Not even that," he said, because Dunican was precisely that kind of asshole. At least he wasn't wearing his aviators, at night, in a darkened room.

I sat across from him at my round dining-room table. It was my father's. Dark, heavy wood and legs that were slightly too long. It made anyone under six feet look a little silly and Dunican was about five-nine.

"Yeah, tell me again why I was let go," I said.

"Well, you released a terrorist. Twice. Right?" he said.

"You mean the terrorist who you announced, just last week, was not a terrorist and is no longer under investigation?"

"Well, that was last week, not six months ago," he said, and I think I may have sneered. Whatever my face did, it felt good. "Don't be like that," he continued. "Why do you think I'm here? We all know you fell on your sword. You did it for the agency like a good soldier. Everyone knows you're one of the good ones."

"You didn't say that when you fired me. You didn't say much of anything."

"Well, that's the gig, right? Discretion is key." I didn't say a word, and he continued on with his peace offering.

"Your only sin, as far as I'm concerned was that you were in a position to be fired. Someone had to be blamed, and you just didn't do a good enough job of making sure it wasn't you."

"That's sweet, Pat. So what brings you here besides pissing in my toilet and putting a cigarette out in my granny's candy dish?"

"I thought that was obvious," he said. "We'd like you to come back."

"What does that mean?"

"Call it a six-month sabbatical," he said. "You've earned it. The blowback has died down. No one gives a shit about Gladstone anymore, and we'd like you back."

"No one cares about Gladstone?"

"Old news," Patrick said.

"Well, Pat, you must know I've been to Australia, right? You're the NSA, you know where I've traveled."

"OK, correction, Aaron. No one cares about Gladstone except *you*. Did you find him, by the way?"

That was the question I'd been waiting for. "No, I didn't find him," I said, "I went over there, but I ended up being a tourist."

"You don't say?" he said.

"Yep. Saw the Sydney Opera House and everything. Did you know it's covered? There's glass over those shells."

"Come home, Aaron. We need you."

"I'm not going back to L.A.," I said.

"We don't want you to," he replied. "You were in L.A. because of Gladstone. The NSA is done with you. Frankly, they may be done with me soon too, and I'll be back to the bureau. The Apocalypse is ending. Slowly. Come back to the FBI like the old days."

I leaned back in my chair and put my hat on the table. Dunican offered his hand. "Whaddya say?"

"Can I take a week to think about it?"

"Sure, sure. I'm here because I respect you. No pressure. You've had six months. What's one more week? Is there anything I can answer for you? Y'know, not as your boss, just man to man?"

I took Pat tightly by the hand and sandwiched it with my other. "No," I said, "I just have to think if I want to work with such a fucking asshole," I said. Then I smiled, because I had to, and he laughed for the same reason.

Day 425

Margo had asked me what it felt like to be home and I couldn't answer. Another day did little to help that. Everything was too quick, too big, too bright, and I was still just a spectator. Even worse, I'd be leaving New York as soon as I'd arrived.

After Central Park, I needed to get away from Hamilton and his angry horde. Jeeves had either betrayed me or put our plan into action before we even delivered it, but both were too intense for me to accept in that moment. I pulled Margo onto a downtown local train still comforted by the thought that no one can get you when you don't stay in one place. I put the time to good use, reading Rowsdower's reports as we crept downtown, learning more about this new version of the man Margo had told me about. He seemed somehow both tougher and more fragile than I could have known, and I hoped his crush on Margo wouldn't get in the way of us being actual friends one day.

As we neared the end of the line, I wondered about procrastinating further by riding back uptown. But somewhere after Rector, she just put her head on my shoulder, and from the reflection in the window opposite us, I could tell she was smiling. Her eyes were closed and she wasn't worrying about me or what came next. All she was doing was feeling my support. As we slowed toward South Ferry, I tucked a tiny bit of hair behind her ear and whispered, "It's time to go, baby."

Outside, the big blue letters for the Staten Island Ferry stood above a terminal of glass and steel, and they still looked like a sign at the entrance of a carnival ride. I took Margo to the only bar on Stone Street not filled with financial douchebags, owing to its lack of both TVs and tube-topped bartenders. I wasn't drinking, but I wanted her to try the fried pickles. Rowsdower was right. She was the kind of person who could have a five-minute conversation about a tomato, and this was the most interesting culinary thing I had to offer. After all, the Growler did their fried pickles as wedges, not slices.

I still wasn't ready to talk about Jeeves. I was just so happy being on an honest-to-goodness date with Margo that everything else seemed like a distraction. We sat at a high-top table against the wall, and I flipped through Rowsdower's reports while sneaking glances at an L.A. girl who made me feel more at home than any of the familiar landmarks.

"I gotta ask you a question," I said while she sipped a

vodka soda with lime. "I get why you had my letters in your suitcase, but why did you have photocopies of *your* letters?"

"That's weird, huh?" she asked.

"A bit, yeah."

"I dunno," she said. "Maybe I wanted our letters to be together if we couldn't be."

I didn't say anything, and, instead, I just kept making my way to the end of Rowsdower's reports.

"You're not buying that?" Margo asked.

"Not really, no."

The pickles came and Margo was excited to note their wedge cut.

"I told you, baby. Only the best." I watched her try one, and then I said, "I think maybe you weren't quite ready to let those letters go."

"Two things," she replied. "One: I *did* let them go. I mailed them. And two: damn, these pickles are good."

"They are," I said, stabbing one with a two-pronged wooden fork. "But I'm not sure keeping copies counts as 'letting go.'"

"Well, if we still had the Internet," she said, "wouldn't what I sent you still be there in my Sent box?"

"It would, and I'm not sure that changes anything." We were silent for a moment and that was OK. Each of us had too much respect for the other to argue too strenuously for anything less than fully formed ideas. "I think I'm ready to talk about Jeeves now," I said finally. "That endorsement's bullshit, right? He's only doing exactly what we were going to ask him to?"

"Well, you know him better, but he certainly *seemed* to be grabbing Hamilton tight."

"Yeah, except there was one thing he said that stuck out. Sounded weird."

"The stuff about you walking on water or looking for porn?" she asked, popping another pickle.

"Yes! Wasn't that just kind of off and mean?"

A young woman sitting behind me, sporting oversized glasses and insanely manicured eyebrows stopped the waitress to ask what music was playing. The waitress looked for the bartender, but I'd heard this iPod playlist traveling through the bar's sound system countless times. "It's 'These Eyes' by the Guess Who," I said, and she replied, "Thank you," which was kind, considering she meant, "Holy fuck, how incredibly old are you?"

"Are you going to keep playing it?" she asked the waitress, "because, I forgot my headphones today and it's getting me a little crazy." She had her Mac out alongside her salad and some red wine.

"Well, it's a playlist," the waitress offered, "so maybe you'll like the rest of the songs better?"

"What's next?" she asked.

I was pretty sure it was Rodriguez from the *Searching for Sugar Man* soundtrack, but I didn't have the heart to tell her.

"Maybe Jeeves was sending a message to us," Margo asked, doing a better job of ignoring the patron. "Referencing something from your journal?"

"Well, there was certainly enough porn in it," I said. "The Rule 34 Club? That's down the street. We could check it out?"

"Is it?"

"Yeah, Beaver Street," I said, and laughed. "Just realized that. How appropriate."

"But it wasn't just the porn," Margo said. "There was that walking-on-water reference too. Maybe something to do with Trinity Church, where Alexander Hamilton's buried? That's in the book and around here too, right?"

"Yeah, but . . ."

Suddenly, Rodriguez came on, and it wasn't what our friend was hoping for.

"No thank you," she said, dropping cash on the table, and I turned around to see if I was missing something. "Remind me to never leave my apartment without headphones again."

"Poor thing," Margo said.

"Yeah, finish your pickles," I said. "I think I know where we're going."

"Off to the Rule 34 Club to request a tone-deaf, twentysomething with on-fleek eyebrows?" Margo offered.

"Oh stop it," I replied. "No. It's the reference to walking on water *and* buying porn. In the book, remember, there's that newspaper stand on Water and Wall?"

"Man, Jeeves is smart."

"Annoyingly so," I said. "Let's go. And if you're good, I'll pick you up a copy of *Inches*."

"You want me to go first?" Margo asked as we walked up Stone toward Water.

"It's fine," I replied. "No one knows I'm here. If anything, they'll be expecting Rowsdower."

We got to the intersection at Wall Street and the newsstand was still there. And just like a year earlier, it was flooded with hard-copy porn, as the Internet had yet to make a reliable return. I looked around for some further clue.

"What are we looking for?" Margo asked.

"That!" I said, and pointed to a bench at an office building across the street. Tobey was sitting outside, and reading one of several magazines he seemingly just purchased.

We crossed Water, and Margo sat alone at the bench opposite Tobey, crossing her legs provocatively enough for him to put his smut down for a moment. Meanwhile, I snuck up behind him, covering his eyes and whispering in his ear, "Six Degrees of Stanley Tucci. *Steel Magnolias*. Go!"

"Gladstone?" he asked, and I growled, "Answer or you're dead."

Tobey started to panic. "Uh, OK, *Steel Magnolias*, uh Dolly Parton! She was in *Rhinestone* with Sylvester Stallone. Stallone was in *Bananas* with Woody Allen. Woody Allen was in *Deconstructing Harry* with Stanley Tucci!"

"Fuck, you did it in three," I said, and took my hands off his eyes.

"Gladstone!" he shouted, and turned around to hug me over the bench.

Then Margo came up behind him and put her hands over his eyes. "First of all, use your inside voice when saying 'Gladstone,'" she ordered. "Also, don't get too excited. You should have picked Julia Roberts from *Steel Magnolias*, and then gone to the *Pelican Brief* with she and Tucci. One step."

"I think I just came," Tobey said, and that did a good job of getting Margo to take her hands off him.

He turned around to see who had just bested him, and upon catching a full look of her he added, "And again."

"Margo," I said, "this is my sexually immature friend, Brendan Tobey. I apologize on his behalf."

"No apologies necessary. I understand that syphilis often attacks the brain if left untreated," she replied while wiping her hands on her skirt.

"And Tobey, this is my friend Margo."

I hadn't called Margo my girlfriend yet, which seemed ridiculous, considering I'd already told her I loved her. It wasn't a lack of feeling. It was just not having lived together long enough in the world.

"Nice to meet you," he said like an actual grown-up, and I came around to the other side of the bench. "Likewise," she replied, and the three of us sat, with Tobey in the middle and his three inches of porn on his lap.

"What are you doing in New York?" I asked.

"I'm crashing with Jeeves. Funny thing about FedEx/Kinkos—they don't keep your job open if you're detained indefinitely under the NET Recovery Act. I was down to my last forty bucks."

"And you just wasted it on eight porno mags?" I asked.

"Fuck yeah," he replied. "There's still no Internet and you don't even want to know what Jeeves has on his shelves."

I cut to the chase. "Jeeves isn't really supporting Hamilton, right? It's a con?"

"Of course," Tobey said. "Burke reached out to him. It was all his idea, but Jeeves just went along to get information because he already suspected something. He's going on a tour with him. New York, Philly, Boston,

Chicago, and L.A. Anointing him as the Internet Messiah all over America while getting his info."

"He's the one, Tobes."

"What one?"

"Hamilton took the Net. He's behind the bombs. He killed Romaya."

"I heard about Romaya," he said, and he reached out, holding onto the back of my neck, his thumb on the side of my face. "I'm sorry about that."

It was the first time since the murder that someone who actually knew Romaya had expressed sympathy to me, and even though I appreciated it, it felt wrong. Hamilton had killed Romaya to hurt me. To destroy me, but the rage I felt in the months that followed was no longer fueled by my loss. After all, I'd mourned Romaya for years before she'd even died, and thinking back to L.A. from the other side of the world, I could see my attempts to rekindle that love were impossible. But my anger grew and grew, not because of what Hamilton took from me but what he took from Romaya—the chance to build a new life without me. Everyone deserves a second chance, and she was having hers until he put an end to it. That was not a crime that could go unpunished like some white-collar fraud settled with a fine. He had to be destroyed.

"I need Jeeves to get Hamilton's collaborators," I said. "Who drove the helicopter? Who pulled the trigger? We can get those names to Anonymous and build a case. Then Rowsdower drops the hammer on him."

"Where's Rowsdower?" Tobey asked, his eyes drifting toward Margo's cleavage. His solemnity was apparently short-lived. "He's the one I was expecting. Jeeves said he got a call from him."

"The NSA was outside his apartment, so he sent us to tell Jeeves the plan instead."

"The one he was already doing?"

"Yeah, apparently," I said. "But again, tell him the kind of people we're looking for so he can focus his energies. And tell him we'll find him in L.A. We have to head back there anyway."

"OK. Anything else you want me to do?" Tobey asked.

"I don't know, Tobes," I said. "Maybe go thirty seconds without staring at my girlfriend's breasts?"

Three hours later, sitting in JFK and waiting for our flight to L.A., Margo took my hand and said, "I liked it when you called me your girlfriend."

"Yeah, well, y'know, Tobey. He just brings out the romantic in me."

Report 10

I knew I was going to take the job. How could I not? Being a fed had been my identity for my entire adult life. But I'd made a promise to help Gladstone, and I liked how I felt seeing it through. Besides, the FBI threw me out at its convenience. It could wait another week to have me back. So I headed to L.A. to reconnect with Stanton. Hopefully, Gladstone and Margo had already met with Jeeves. It certainly seemed like it, the way he was criss-crossing America, anointing Burke the new Messiah, holding hands at every stop.

Gladstone had the hard copies of my reports, but I read them over on my laptop as I headed west, cringing over the parts that revealed my crush on Margo, but more important, noticing something obvious I'd missed: Neville. Based on what we knew, he was the only conduit to Hamilton Burke regarding Gladstone's story about the dollar-store dad. And if he'd given Burke that, what else had he given as an ICANN crypto officer?

I wasn't the only one asking about ICANN's activities. The news was filled with reports of Michiko Nagasoto's murder, casting a further cloud over the administration that had just tasked this international community to do a full-scale Internet audit. The hubs were all intact and staying that way. The plumbing of the Internet was all functional, but very few sites could be reached. The Internet, we were told, was coming back, but literally one site at a time, after each was ICANN approved and allowed through its security protocols. It wasn't something the people were happy about even without Burke playing savior/agitator as the new and improved Internet Messiah. People were protesting. Gladstone's symbol was everywhere with all the usual messages: BRING BACK OUR INTERNET, THE INTERNET IS PEOPLE AND WE'RE STILL HERE, and even BRING GLADSTONE HOME. And despite what she claimed to be a slim profit margin, Margo had to be making a killing with those Gladstone masks. More and more, the protests were filled with people in those cheap felt fedoras and half faceplates. Now they numbered even more than the Guy Fawkes masks in the crowd.

I called Stanton's L.A. landline from the airport and his messaging service had a car bring me to the Chateau Marmont. Apparently, he was renting the penthouse indefinitely. At the hotel, everything was taken care of and I felt a level of respect I wasn't used to. I was accustomed to gratuitous "sir"s and smiles. Those came from fear. The world becomes polite inches from the fire. But these stumbling attendants and valets weren't afraid. They truly believed I held some sort of significance. I was rich. I was influential. I was a personal guest of Reginald Stanton. Mr. Stanton is expecting me. Mr. Stanton said to give me whatever I needed. I was living in rarefied air, and I couldn't breathe because none of it felt like my country. But I still hoped the cash I had on me to tip my cleanly shaved personal guide to Stanton's suite could keep the misperception of my importance going.

"I think I got it from here," I said, standing outside the door and handing him a five. It was either that or give the twenty, and I didn't care about being mistaken for important enough to do that.

"Very well, sir," the young man said, sticking the cash in his pocket without looking, but he didn't leave. Instead, he knocked clean and hard, announcing, "Mr. Stanton, your guest has arrived."

Stanton threw open the door. "Rowsdower!" he shouted. "Get in here, ya dirty ol' prick!" He handed the bellhop a twenty and pulled me into what was quite simply the sunniest hotel room I'd ever seen. Fully furnished like the nicest private home, leading out to an immense balcony overlooking the Hollywood Hills. We weren't alone. There was a man on the balcony with his back to me, dressed in that kind of California business casual I was never able to effectuate.

"We're not alone?" I asked.

"Oi!" he shouted, putting his arm around me and leading me out to the terrace. "We've got company!"

The man outside turned around, and I said his name before I even realized I was speaking. "Professor Leonards," I said. "What are you doing here?"

"He's Michiko's replacement," Stanton said.

"You guys are fucking?" I asked, and Leonards laughed that great gravelly laugh he had.

"Fuck off," Stanton said, giving me a shove. "He's a crypto officer now."

"I know, Reg. It was a bad joke. I'm sorry."

"Sounded more like Gladstone than you," Leonards said. "Must be the hat."

"Professor Leonards," I said, shaking his hand, "it's a pleasure to see you again."

Stanton called us over to the outdoor bar and we sat on stools while he played bartender, a role he apparently relished.

"What'll it be, lads?" he asked.

I said I'd take a Johnnie Walker on the rocks and Leonards opted for some white wine.

"Good, good," Stanton replied, pouring liquors seemingly at random into a blender. "Koala Fuckers all around then!" he shouted, and flipped the switch.

Leonards looked to me for an explanation. "It was really an act of pure optimism to give our orders in the first place," I said.

Stanton must have required that his penthouse bar be stocked with all the Koala Fucker essentials, because he dished out the drinks, replete with Krazy Straws.

I tried to get down to business. "Gentlemen," I said, "as you both know, I'm no computer scholar, but this Internet audit . . . from one to ten, how much of a load of shit is it?"

Leonards enjoyed the question immensely. "How do you mean?" he asked.

"Well, who's first on the list to return?" I asked.

"After two days of intense ICANN meetings," he replied, "it seems Microsoft Outlook and Google are at the top of the list to return. Their security protocols are being audited now and I expect they should be cleared tomorrow."

"So the two big Internet behemoths just coincidentally have the influence to go first?"

Stanton put down his drink to interject. "Well, it's not just money," he said. "Why do you think they're so rich? Think of all their users. It's in the public's interest."

Leonards watched me, and even though he was nothing like my father, it was enough to make me remember what it felt like to be someone's son.

"Wait a second," I said. "What good is bringing back Google if all the sites you could use it to search for are still down?" Leonards was liking me more and more. "And what about news?" I continued. "Who's top of the list to come back?"

"CNN," Leonards replied. "Problem with that?" It wasn't a question. It was a test.

"Well, it certainly seems a bit convenient that the news organization friendliest to this administration is the first to come back, right? Who knows how long before any other comes back? I can't believe you're OK with all this."

"Who said I'm OK with it?" Leonards asked. "But I've only just got here. When Michiko was murdered, they needed a crypto officer who would meet with unanimous approval so nothing slowed down the audit."

"And the father of the Internet was the obvious choice?"

"I really like the way you remember everything, Aaron," he said. "So what else can we tell you?"

"What about all the apps? When can we expect those?"

"Tell him, Reginald," Leonards directed, and Stanton turned a little sheepish, which is something I'd not seen him be yet.

"Well, there's an app called PeepHole launching with Google, Microsoft Office, and CNN this week."

"People?" I asked.

"No. PeepHole," he corrected.

"Sounds pornographic."

Leonards laughed again. "That's what I said! Tell him about it, Reggie."

"Well, *PeepHole*, which is not pornographic, turns your phone into a video camera. You can broadcast yourself and where you are like you're the star of your own little reality show. The video is uploaded to a server and deleted after twenty-four hours."

I was no expert, but this didn't sound nearly as novel as Stanton was trying to make it. "Isn't there already an app like that?" I asked.

"Several," Leonards said. "But actually none, because they're all offline now, right? So the owner of PeepHole sure is one lucky guy. He'll make a killing!"

"Who's that?" I asked, being slow on the uptake. Leonards pointed to Stanton.

"Don't give me that look," Stanton said. "I'm a very good security risk. It makes sense to clear me first. I'm a crypto officer. Besides, releasing my new app is a safe way to give something to the people. And if my app happens to get a foothold in the market during the Apocalypse because of it, so be it. Also, mine's different because it also allows viewers to download others' broadcasts to their phones."

Leonards put his drink down on the bar. "And so, Special Agent Rowsdower," he said, "in answer to your question, all things considered, I'd put the load-of-shit rating on this ICANN audit at about a five. Of course, money, power, and corruption—all the usual players— are definitely influencing who comes to the top of the audit and how quickly, but I will say this: The threat is real. Multiple times now, forces have penetrated DNS-SEC's protocols. That's not invented, and it can't be allowed to happen. There are bad guys."

"Right," said Stanton. "And isn't that why you're here, Rowsdower? What have you got for us?"

I paused and took a long draw on my Koala Fucker, watching the wretched mix slowly twist through my Krazy Straw. And it wasn't just to torture Stanton by keeping him waiting, but because I still had things to investigate. I had encouraged Gladstone to leave his safe Australian cave and he placed his faith in me by doing so. Maybe more so in Margo, but if I were going to divulge anything about him I had to be sure. I now had more information about ICANN's activities than when I'd arrived, and more distrust. I didn't bother hiding my suspicions and Stanton came around from the bar and stood beside me.

"It's OK, Rowsdower," he said. "I knew you thought we'd be alone today, and you're a careful man. That's good. If you need to interrogate Leonards a bit before speaking, go ahead."

"Well, there is something I need to know from the

professor before I speak any further," I said. Leonards swiveled himself directly toward me. "Professor," I said, "can I trust Stanton?"

Leonards laughed as I hoped he would. Not just for the misdirect he clearly appreciated, but because he approved of my skepticism. "Yes, I think so," he said. "Stanton's just a capitalist through and through. He can't help it, but he's not the bad guy."

I remembered what Margo had told me—If you're going to save the world, you better make it profitable—and decided it was safe to speak.

"It's Hamilton Burke," I said.

"Hamilton Burke what?" Stanton asked.

"He's the one who took the Net, did the bombings, killed Gladstone's ex, and, I think Michiko too."

"Why would he do that?" Leonards asked.

"I'm working on it."

"What about Gladstone?" Stanton asked.

"He's safe," I said. "Now, answer my questions. Whoever's penetrating ICANN's security protocols needs a mole on the inside, right?"

"It would help," Leonards said.

"Meaning someone who knew the code to all the security protocols could help an outsider get around them, play havoc with the Net?"

"Right," Stanton said. "So?"

"So where's your third keymaster?" Where's Neville Bhattacharyya?"

Leonards and Stanton exchanged looks. "He wasn't feeling well, and declined our invitation," Leonards said.

"Stanton, when Margo and I met you, we tried to tell you that story about the dollar-store dad, but you'd already heard it from Burke, remember? Well, we told that story to Bhattacharyya before Burke started using it. You say Bhattacharyya's sick; I've seen his old photos. Now, he looks more like he's dying. And he's got kids."

"You're saying he's susceptible to bribery? A millionaire?" Leonards asked.

"Millionaire, my arse," Stanton replied. "Tech Global lost everything two years ago, remember? Hostile takeover. Hargazian runs that company now. Bhattacharyya's pretty much a figurehead for marketing. He's on salary."

Leonards shrugged. "I defer to the capitalist," he said. "They're better at getting into the heads of their own kind."

"With all due respect, Professor," I said. "I'm betting on you being wrong."

Day 428

Margo and I flew into L.A. the night before meeting Jeeves and stayed in a shitty little Santa Monica hotel. Given that Tobey had no money to spend on weed, I was confident he'd deliver our messages to Jeeves. First, in person, telling him what kind of information to pull from Burke's mind, and later, providing the L.A. meeting place to exchange that information after his Internet Messiah speaking tour was over.

That night, even though we flipped the mattress looking for bed bugs before we dared get under the covers, I felt safer than I had in months. I held Margo hard and tight around her middle and she wrapped her long arms around me. I don't want to tell you about our sex. I don't want to write it down, because there is only one other person I want to make sure understands how I feel, and she already knows. But I will say in the past, I'd run to sex as an escape from stress, from loneliness. And in good times, I'd felt excitement and love, and even all the titillation the dirty adult world had promised to me as an addescent, but the difference with Margo was that sleeping with her just made me happy. There was nowhere else to go. Nothing left to do. No more to feel.

The next day we took the Pacific Coast Highway to a seafood place called Neptune's Net that Margo picked because it was out of the way and too boorish for Burke's tastes in case I still had any fear of bumping into him. (She also said it would make a cool locale for the movie.) We'd left the hotel with plenty of time for our six thirty p.m. meeting, but there must have been an accident because the highway slowly snaked for miles between the Pacific Ocean and the Santa Monica Mountains. I was afraid we'd be late, but Margo explained the highway was the only way to get where we were going, so Jeeves was probably stuck too.

We arrived at seven and after poking our heads inside to make sure Jeeves wasn't already there, we took a seat on the deck outside. We wanted to catch him on the way in, and frankly part of me still wanted to watch for anyone coming. The place was filled with bikers and bicyclists, each dressed accordingly, and it was hard not to imagine some sort of fight breaking out with each team so easily identified by dress. It was also hard not to imagine the bicyclists getting their asses kicked.

The sun was setting over the Pacific in a way I'd never seen.

"The water looks almost golden," I said.

"Well, yeah, that's why they call it the Golden State," Margo replied.

"I thought that was because of the gold rush."

"I used to think that too," she said while flipping through the menu, but she put it down almost instantly to stare over my shoulder. It was Jeeves, and he must have come directly from a Hamilton engagement because he was still wearing crisp khaki shorts and a button-down shirt. He smiled when he saw me, but it looked like it hurt. Something was wrong. Maybe it's because I wasn't alone. He came over to our table, stopping on Margo's side first.

"Dan," I said. "This is Margo Zmena, she—" but I didn't get to finish, because he grabbed Margo's extended hand and sandwiched it tightly between his own, and when Margo decided to pretend it was still a normal handshake and bring it to an end, Dan wouldn't let her go. He held tight and closed his eyes, almost shaking with concentration as a tiny smile slowly spread across his face. Then bigger and bigger until he released her.

"I'm sorry," he said. "I'm just a little overprotective." Then he gently touched Margo's face, no longer looking for answers, just wanting to appreciate what he'd found. "Thank you," he said, and I could see he was almost crying. I opened my arms, and he edged his way around the table, and now he really was crying.

"I'm so sorry, Gladstone," he said, holding my face in his hands.

"What for?" I asked.

"For everything. I know what he did to you. I saw everything."

"Hamilton?"

"Yes," Jeeves said, wrapping his arms around me and squeezing. "I'm so sorry, Wayne."

"It's OK, Dan," I said. "I'm OK. Please, let's sit."

We spent the next few minutes nearly silent. Jeeves needed the time. We sat and watched the sun go from gold to gone before ordering drinks. Jeeves ran his finger around the ribbon of my fedora sitting on the table. I told him it was a gift from Margo and once belonged to David Bowie. He told me he knew. When the drinks came, Jeeves knocked back half his beer before reaching into his shirt pocket and pulling out a flash drive.

"This has just one document," he said, "but it's everything I pulled from Hamilton. Every name I could see. Every physical description I could muster. Every bank-account number. Gunmen, pilots, everything."

I took the flash drive and put it in my pocket, thinking about what it must have been like for a good man like Jeeves to live in Hamilton's mind for a full week. "I'm sorry, Dan," I said, putting my hand on his. "Thank you." He drank from his Anchor Steam more leisurely, but he still wasn't the man I remembered, so I pulled out a five and put it on the table.

"Hey, Jeeves," I said. "Why do they call California the Golden State?"

"Well, there's a fair amount of debate over that actually. Many say because of the gold rush, but then there are the golden sunsets over the Pacific. The state colors are gold and blue, there are the golden poppies, and, of course, the Golden Gate Bridge, so y'know, pick one."

"There's my Jeeves," I said. "Keep the five, big guy. You earned it."

Margo smiled, happy that she got to see a display of Jeeves's old Central Park stylings, but I could tell she had questions. "So Dan," Margo said, "if you're up to it, I do have some questions."

Jeeves wasn't quite up to answers, but he understood the need for questions. "Go ahead," he said.

"So you found information on accomplices, and that's exactly what Rowsdower asked for, but did you get any, I don't know, insight? What are Hamilton's motives?"

You didn't need to be a psychic to know that was the question anyone would have. Jeeves finished his beer in a long, slow swig, eyeing my plain seltzer. "Good for you, Wayne," he said before turning back to Margo. "That was the hardest part," he said. "I kept holding on, even prepping him to think about his motivations before each incidental touch, and all I can tell you is . . ." Jeeves stopped. "Someone's coming."

Margo didn't wait. She grabbed Jeeves's empty beer bottle and cracked it on the wooden railing to her left, pieces of broken glass falling down on the grass below. I dug the flash drive deeper into my jeans pocket. "Easy," Jeeves said. "It's just Rowsdower."

Rowsdower was dressed in his old gray suit, wearing an impossibly thin black tie and my grandfather's fedora. He spotted us instantly, and was pissed.

"Jesus fucking Christ," he said. "The traffic in this fucking bullshit city!" He sat down next to Margo, opposite Jeeves, and flagged a passing waitress with red hair. "Johnnie Walker, rocks," he said. "Thanks."

The waitress broke stride for a moment to acknowledge the order and give Margo a disapproving look. "It's usually the bikers who start breaking bottles," she said.

"I'm sorry, Sage," Margo said, noting the name tag. "I left my leather jacket at home."

"How'd you know where to find us?" I asked Rowsdower.

"How ya think? Tobey," he replied.

"Good point. And what happened with the NSA?" I asked. "Is everything all right?"

"Yeah, they offered me my job back. Well, to the FBI, more specifically."

"That's great, Aaron," Margo said. "So you really were just collateral damage?" she asked, clearly referencing their conversation I knew only from Rowsdower's reports.

"Seems that way," he said. "They want me back at the bureau now that the NET Recovery Act's allegedly winding down and Gladstone here is no longer enemy number one."

"Are you taking it?" Jeeves asked.

"Not yet," he said. "We have business to take care of first."

Jeeves was pleased to hear that. "I pulled every single accomplice name I could and put it all on a flash drive I gave to Gladstone," he said.

Rowsdower looked me over, noting I had no shirt pockets or backpack. He knew the drive was in my jeans. "Was Neville Bhattacharyya one of them?" he asked, and Jeeves showed the surprise so often reserved for his audience's face. Rowsdower was happier than I'd ever seen him.

"How did you know?" Jeeves asked.

Margo put her hand on Rowsdower's shoulder and said, "Because it's his job to know."

"Yes, Neville and a lot more," Jeeves said, "but when you arrived, we were moving from means to motive."

"Before we get to that," Margo said. "Something's bothering me. Hamilton read Gladstone's book. He heard all about you, Jeeves. Why would a man with so much to hide put himself in a position to be seen by you so many times?"

"He doesn't believe in me," Jeeves said.

"Because he's a bottom line, hard-nosed business-man? That sort of thing?" Rowsdower asked.

"It's not just a lack of faith, but humility," Jeeves said." I proclaimed Gladstone the Internet Messiah, and as far as he's concerned I'm wrong. He thinks Gladstone's dead or drinking himself to death somewhere in the world. Hamilton believes in himself far more than any prophecy, and he's very pleased about destroying Glad-stone."

Hamilton had told me he needed me out of the way without murder because the movement would only grow with a martyr. That made sense, but I still wanted to ask again. "Why did he need to destroy me?"

My question returned all the pain my Golden State trivia had relieved, and Jeeves closed his eyes as if suf-fering a burn without screaming. I was making him re-member. "Because," he said, almost mastering the quiver in his voice, "he hates you."

No one spoke for a moment. There was nothing left of the sun. The tables were lit by electric lights above, which obscured any effect of each table's tiny flickering candle. I tried to understand why being hated by a mon-ster I despised was enough to make me feel sad and frightened.

"But Wayne," Jeeves said, "he also kind of loves you. I mean, he wants to become the Internet Messiah."

"That's what Margo said," I replied.

"Think of that," Jeeves continued. "This man who has

succeeded at every financial endeavor in life, who can buy and sell all of us a hundred times over—the only thing he wanted, the only thing he didn't have is what you have: tons of followers believing in a cause."

"So he took the Internet away just so he could bring it back?" Rowsdower asked.

"There's no one answer," Jeeves explained. "Having conquered the world, I believe boredom is a very big motivator for him these days, and I also think what he said to Gladstone at Trinity Church was true. First it was magnanimous—help the workingman by removing the tool that disproportionately increased the expectations of productivity. Then he thought maybe he could profit from bringing it back, but ultimately, he just wanted to be a hero. To be a champion of pure things."

"Even if he had to steal, murder, and destroy to do it," I said.

"Yes," Jeeves agreed. "And with each cyberattack, each bomb, each murder, the administration became more and more oppressive. They became the bad guy for him to rail against."

"He made the government his unwitting collaborator," Margo said.

"Right," Jeeves said. "And that pleased him immensely."

"Well," Rowsdower said. "Seems he's a lot like you already, right Gladstone?"

"Meaning what?" I asked.

"Well, you had me running all over the world with clues to find you, not knowing I was only serving your purposes."

"How?"

"Whaddya mean? You had Margo and me meeting all

the ICANN Internet power brokers, singing the gospel of Gladstone, telling your dollar-store story."

"Yeah, that was Margo's idea. I didn't even know what ICANN was until her, but I was afraid for her to go alone, and I wasn't ready to leave the first safe spot I found in years."

Rowsdower backed off a bit, because only animals and the worst humans attack when they smell fear.

"But more importantly," I continued, "I trusted you."

"To play bodyguard?"

"No. To do whatever needed to be done. I had faith that if you met with some of the most important people of the Internet, you'd figure out what was needed in a way I never could. You and Margo both."

"You really didn't have more of a plan than that?" Rowsdower asked.

"No." I laughed. "Blame this asshole," I said, pointing to Jeeves. "He started it." Jeeves put his hand over mine on the table and held it there.

"It's worked so far," he said.

"I just kept finding people I trusted and kept believing."

"Well, speaking of that," Rowsdower said. "Give me the flash drive. I'm meeting with Anonymous tomorrow."

"The same contact?" Margo asked.

"Yeah, the black guy."

No one spoke.

"What? He's black. What should I call him, the guy who dresses like Guy Fawkes? That won't really help."

"How about just his name?" Jeeves asked.

"He doesn't have a name," Rowsdower said. "He's *Anonymous.*"

"Black Fawkes Down?" I offered.

"How is that better?" Rowsdower asked.

"You could have just said 'yes' and left it at that," Margo said.

"Fine," Rowsdower said. "Yes. The same contact at Anonymous. The one who I've decided to trust because he got the information that got Jeeves and Tobey out of prison. That one. OK?"

"What can Anonymous do with the Internet down?" Jeeves asked.

"It's not down," Rowsdower replied. "Unlike before, the hubs are operational. The world is connected, but ICANN is eking out the working sites, making them pass their audits. Each week, they're going to update the DNS-SEC protocols to allow in more approved sites."

I wanted to cough "nerd," but Tobey wasn't there and he was the only person I knew who'd laugh at that.

"Which brings me to the gift-giving part of the show," Rowsdower continued, and pulled some folded papers out of his left inside coat pocket. "Everything I just told you is in my last report. I wanted you to have it to keep with the others." He slid the papers across the table and then reached into his right coat pocket and pulled out an iPhone Infinity. "I got you a present," he said, handing it to me. "Next week, there will be more, but right now, you've got a phone with the one working app on the Internet. PeepHole."

"People?" I asked.

"No, *PeepHole.*"

"What is that? Some sort of sex thing?"

"No, it lets you broadcast yourself like the star of your own little reality show. Just do me a favor. Keep it on your phone, OK? And another favor, give me the flash drive."

Rowsdower held his hand palm open on the table, and I reached into my pocket with enough hesitation for him to notice.

"Give me one week," he said. "One week to take Jeeves's impressions and turn them into the evidence against Hamilton we need. We can bust him."

I placed the drive in Rowsdower's hand, but before he could close his fingers, Jeeves covered the drive with his palm. He squeezed Rowsdower's hand and closed his eyes. Rowsdower did not fight, and after a moment, Jeeves opened his eyes with a start and stared right at him.

"Are you sure about what you're walking into, Aaron?" he said.

"No, I'm not," Rowsdower replied. "But you know what they say: miracles and disasters look the same in the distance."

Day 434

Margo took me to her place in La Brea, and as we drove down Wilshire Boulevard, neither the sun nor the palm trees nor the smiles bothered me as they had before. They didn't look like distractions from work, because our work, for the moment, was waiting. Rowsdower had the intel, Anonymous was finding documents, and from their work Rowsdower would build the criminal case against Burke. Murder, terrorism, cyberterrorism. All I had to do was wait for Hamilton to be destroyed.

When we pulled up to Margo's place, I was confused, because it looked like the white palatial estate of a 1940s movie star, with all its Spanish tile and white arches.

"You live here?" I asked.

"It's not a mansion," she said. "You'll see."

We went through the front door, which opened to a main lobby, where Margo picked up her mail. Then she took me through a back door directly opposite the one we'd entered to show me a huge green courtyard. It seemed this place really was a mansion once, but it had been gutted. The center was now a lawn, replete with a fountain. There were rows of apartments along both sides.

"Not what you were expecting, huh?" Margo said.

"Yeah, I had no idea I was dating one of the chicks from *Melrose Place*."

Inside, Margo's apartment was modest and it reminded me a lot of mine in Australia. Lots of white, lots of light, and plenty of hardwood floors. It was clean with minimal clutter with the exception of Margo's old CDs that lined all her window casements. They'd probably been sitting there since she moved in ten years ago. She hadn't moved as she rose up with Rubinek, and even when she got the inheritance money, she kept her needs simple.

Each morning, I woke wrapped up in Margo inside this white, well-lit space that increasingly was starting to feel too much like heaven. On the sixth effortless morning, I decided to inspect the window CDs on my way back from the bathroom. It was an eclectic mix, but most seemed like rejects from the *Garden State* soundtrack.

"Big *Pitchfork* fan, huh?" I said to Margo in place of "Good morning."

"No one's making you listen to them," she said, more annoyed than I expected or intended.

I got back into bed, swaddling her in the comforter on both sides as I lay on top. "Don't be mad," I said. "Being teased by people who love you is good for the soul."

"Yeah?" she asked, looking up at me.

"Definitely."

"Why?"

I wasn't sure. I'd always just assumed it to be true. "I'll think about that," I said, and kissed her nose. "I'm sorry."

We turned on the TV. It seemed her apartment had the same boosted antennae signal as Rowsdower's so the reception was fine. The latest report was that the major cable providers wouldn't be online for another few weeks of audits, and the protests had only intensified. Some led by Burke, some by Anonymous, and some by fans of my book, holding Wi-Fi symbol protest signs. I was biased, but I liked how those guys dressed the best—sports jackets and fedoras, sometimes wearing Margo's Gladstone mask.

"Wish those masks looked a little more like me," I said to Margo.

"Why?" she asked. "Need something to masturbate to?"

I shot out a laugh, and said, "See? It's good for the soul because you shouldn't take yourself too seriously." She pondered the validity of my point for a moment before I added, "Now, enough joking around; let's focus on me being the Messiah."

It turns out my timing was pretty good, because the news cut to a portion of Hamilton's latest speech from the day before. He was outside of the Liberty Bell in Philadelphia.

"Damn, he's good at branding," Margo said.

Hamilton might have not believed in Jeeves, but being anointed certainly did something for him. He spoke even more passionately than before. "The Internet, the government says, is returning. Little by little. *Incremental change*, they say."

Boos rose up from the crowd.

"And why incremental?" he asked. "After all, the hubs are secure. The connections are set, the waves are in the air." He pointed as if he could see them. "But this administration claims additional security is needed. So ICANN, an international committee—that oh, by the way, just happens to answer to the US Department of Commerce— is doing their audit. Anyone here trust that audit?"

The crowd gave Hamilton all the nooooooos he wanted, and it let him up his showmanship. "Oh, come on, friends," he said. "Why be so cynical? Why would you have any reason to doubt this audit? After all, even the conservative *Drudge Report* is for it. Oh, wait, it's not. Drudge hasn't passed his audit and isn't online. But I'm sure the liberal site *Daily Kos* is in favor of it. Oh, wait, they're not online either. Fox is offline. MSNBC is offline. Right now, all we have is CNN, and wouldn't you know it? CNN can't stop praising the president for solving the Apocalypse problem. What were the odds?"

Hamilton interrupted the crowd's laughter to ask, "Does the Internet Apocalypse feel solved to you?" The crowd was angry, but when he followed up with "Do you feel free?" their roar was like a wave breaking. He paced a few steps behind his podium, overseeing his people, before returning and pointing behind him. "We stand here today, in front of a two-hundred-and-fifty-year-old bell, cracked and broken, but if we had the courage, or inclination, to string it up from the highest tower, it would still ring. People could still hear the sound of freedom for miles and miles. Sometimes it would sound strong and sometimes it would sound thin and shrill, but it would ring.

"But is that what this administration does when confronted with broken things? No. It takes control of them, and it meters out the sounds it thinks *we the people* should hear."

"He's right," Margo said.

"Of course he's right," I said. "All the best lies have the benefit of being true."

"I'm asking for your support," Hamilton said. "Make me your president and I'll bring you back a real, unfettered Internet. God bless you, and God bless America!"

Margo shut off the TV and tried to take my hand to offer support in the face of my enemy, but I didn't want sympathy. I didn't want to be coddled. I wanted to fight, and short of that, I wanted the moving parts of my loose collective to hurry up and come together to destroy a monster.

"Do you hear that?" Margo asked, and I listened again. It was some sort of a beep coming from her desk, where I'd left Rowsdower's phone gift to me charging. A push notification from that PeepHole app was letting me know that MessiahFanMan—the only person I followed—was now broadcasting. I tapped the screen, and there he was, my old persecutor, friend, and savior. He was dressed in his typical 1965 G-man style, but he was no longer wearing my grandfather's fedora. He seemed to be broadcasting from the couch of a living room.

"Good afternoon," he said to the phone he was holding directly in front of his face. "My name is Aaron N. Rowsdower, formerly of the Federal Bureau of Investigation and the NSA. I was a foot soldier of the NET Recovery

Act, tasked with finding out who stole the Internet. I've collected that data, and today, I bring it to the FBI. I've asked my former boss, Patrick Dunican, to meet me here, at his Long Island home, because I had news too sensitive to be said within government walls."

"What the fuck is he doing?" I asked Margo, who was looking more concerned than I'd ever seen her.

Rowsdower glared over his left shoulder through what appeared to be a bay window. "Yep, seems he's on his way now." Rowsdower sat back on the couch and then appeared to put the camera in his front jacket pocket facing out. He must have cut some sort of a hole, because a few shreds of fabric obscured the lens.

"Why is he making this public?" I said. "I thought he wanted to build a case."

Margo was on her iPhone. "Well, he's not exactly making it public," she said. "You're the only person who follows him. He has no other posts. Not sure anyone's watching. . . . Oh, and he's marked his account private so only his followers can see. So yeah, just you."

Rowsdower turned to the door as it opened, and Patrick Dunican, wearing those aviators Rowsdower hated so much, entered his home.

"Good afternoon, Patrick," Rowsdower said, but Dunican was too smooth to show surprise.

"Afternoon, Aaron," he said. "Figured you'd already come inside when I saw you weren't in your car."

"Yeah, sorry about that," Rowsdower replied. "I needed to take a leak and besides, your locks are kinda shit."

Dunican sat down at a chair to the side of the couch. "So Aaron, have you come to accept my offer?"

"I have, Pat. Guess I should get used to calling you ADIC Dunican like old times."

"Probably a good idea," Dunican replied, and took out a Camel Light.

"Could I trouble you for one of those?" Rowsdower asked.

"Thought you'd quit," Dunican said. "I didn't see any ashtrays in your apartment."

"I had, but y'know, special occasion, return to work, all that."

The camera went out of frame as Rowsdower lit up and exhaled, but then he turned himself squarely to Dunican again. "Before I return," he said, "if I could deliver evidence on who was responsible for the cyberattacks against the Internet, for the bombings at Farmers Market, the Hollywood sign, and others, and who murdered both Gladstone's ex-wife and former ICANN crypto officer Michiko Nagasoto, would the government be interested?"

Dunican laughed. "What kind of a ridiculous question is that? Of course!"

"No," Rowsdower continued. "When I say interested, I don't just mean curious. I mean would the federal government prosecute the cyberterrorism, would state government prosecute the criminal acts?"

"Why wouldn't they?"

"Because it's big, Pat. It's not some Third World combatant, it's not some rogue superpower or disgruntled former CIA. We're dealing with an incredibly powerful man and multiple people on the take. At least one of the ICANN crypto officers for certain."

"Who is this man?"

"Hamilton Burke."

Dunican stood up and looked out his window.

"You don't seem surprised," Rowsdower said.

"Why should I be? We've been heading an investigation for over a year. There's been talk, but we've never been able to get anything concrete on Hamilton Burke. Can you really nail him?"

"I can," Rowsdower said, and took a flash drive from his pocket, framing it in the same shot with Dunican. It wasn't the flash drive I got from Jeeves, but it didn't need to be. If Anonymous had done its job, it was a drive containing concrete documents and evidence tying Burke to each of his collaborators and actions, not just Jeeves's thoughts and impressions.

"Who'd you get that from? Gladstone?" Dunican asked.

"I told you, Pat. I don't know where Gladstone is. This came from Anonymous."

"You're shitting me."

"Well, y'know, when I didn't have a job, I had to make new friends."

"You sure did," he said, and moved farther from Rowsdower. He leaned against the desk on the opposite side of the room.

"This isn't right," I said.

"I can't believe it," Dunican laughed. "A straightlaced guy like you. Special Agent Aaron N. Rowsdower spent his sabbatical as an agent of Anonymous."

"I wouldn't go that far, Pat, but you know me well enough to know I get my man."

"I know you, Aaron. And I know you took shit for twenty years rising just high enough to be known in the bureau as being really good at taking shit. And when we needed you to fall, you fell, and when we asked you back, you came. But you're no dummy, so what I can't figure out is why you didn't realize breaking into my home gave me probable cause to kill you."

Dunican pulled his gun from his holster and fired almost directly at the camera, and I dropped my phone like I was being shot. Rowsdower must have fallen from the couch onto his back because the camera turned to the ceiling and then slid out and over his shoulder to the floor. Rowsdower's ear went in and out of the frame and Dunican came into view, kneeling over Rowsdower's body. Somehow, only hearing Aaron made it worse. The blood in his breathing.

"You stupid shit," Dunican said. "Do you know how easy this will be for me? Disgruntled, disgraced employee, consorting with Anonymous, breaks into my home. It's almost like you wanted me to kill you."

The gurgling became worse because Aaron must have been trying to speak. And he did. "Yeah, almost," he said, and then his bloody hand reached over the phone, and there was Rowsdower, looking right at me, dying. Blood in his otherwise perfectly normal teeth. "Download," he said, and when he tried to smile more blood leaked from the corner of his mouth.

Days 435–436

The fists I made the moment Rowsdower was shot only tightened, and the intensity of it radiated up through my whole body as it shook with the muscle memory of Romaya's loss. It made me so tight and hard that no grief could enter for the moment. There was too much rage, and Margo made a sound I'd never heard before, panicked gasps cutting the wailing. She was saying something I couldn't understand, and she tried to say it again before grabbing the phone and tapping the screen. She watched and waited. Then she tapped it again.

"Download," she said, and dropped the phone back on the bed. She'd saved the footage. It no longer lived only on PeepHole's twenty-four-hour server; I had it in my phone. I went to Margo's Mac on her desk and copied it to her hard drive.

"Now it's in two places," I said.

Margo got up and went to the closet without speaking to me, pulled out a suitcase, and threw it on the bed.

"Where you going?"

"We," she said, pushing tears off her cheeks with the base of her palm. "I'm sure hitting Download will give our GPS location on the phone."

I hadn't thought of that. That's what over a year off the grid does to you. Makes you believe you can ever be alone. "Well, we had to push it anyway before it could be deleted off the server, or at least the Internet shut down again?"

"Right." Margo went over to her laptop to copy the footage again onto a flash drive. "Fucking Macs," she said. "One tear and the whole thing will probably short circuit." Then she turned and looked at me for the first time since the broadcast. "You're not crying," she said.

I walked over to Margo and, seeing her tears, took a deep breath and used all my strength to unfurl my fist before I could gently wipe them from her face. "I don't have the time to cry," I said.

"Oh, Parker," she replied. "You have to learn how to multitask."

I held her for a moment. I thought we could spare it. Besides, if I was wrong, this seemed like a pretty good place to die. But that's when her apartment buzzer rang, and we both jumped. "No one could get here that quick," Margo said, and went to the Intercom by the front door to answer.

"Oi, special delivery from Reginald Stanton."

I only knew Stanton from Rowsdower's reports. "Does that sound like him?" I asked.

"Maybe?" Margo replied.

I pressed the Intercom. "If this is really Reginald Stanton," I said, "then what's the password?"

"Get fucked. That's the password, mate."

"Yeah, that's him," Margo said, and buzzed him in. He was at the door a minute later and after double-checking that he was alone, Margo let him in. He was carrying a square box.

"Special delivery," he said to Margo. "Rowsdower sent this to me with instructions to deliver it to you."

Then Stanton noticed the tears and turned to me. "What'd you do to her?"

"Watch yourself, Gladstone," she said. "He bites."

Stanton dropped the box. "You're Gladstone?"

"Pleased to meet you," I said, shaking his hand, "but we've suffered a bit of a loss today. Rowsdower's been murdered."

Margo called Stanton into her bedroom and replayed the PeepHole transmission from her laptop, knowing neither of us had the energy to explain. She hit Play and left.

"Fuck me," Stanton said when it was over, and Margo returned with a long bread knife and handed it to me. "I'm sure the package is for you," she said.

Stanton placed the box on the hardwood floor and we sat around it as I ran the knife along the sealing tape. Inside, there was an envelope, a flash drive, and a hat. I opened the envelope and read the letter out loud.

Dear Internet Messiah,
As you read this, I might once again be Special Agent
Rowsdower of the Federal Bureau of Investigation, work-

ing within the system to bring down terrorist, murderer, and presidential candidate Hamilton Burke. If so, great! Good for me. But if not, I'm dead, and I have a feeling it's probably the latter, so I have a few things I need to explain.

First, Anonymous came through like a champ. The flash drive containing all documentary evidence of Hamilton Burke, his contacts, his monetary transactions, and even some surveillance footage pulled from security cameras, is all on the flash drive in this box. That is NOT what I showed Dunican. If you're curious, I can tell you what Pat will see when he plays that flash drive is video of me having sex with his ex-wife, Vicki. (She was always kind of sweet on me, and well, I wanted to go out with a bang.) But the point, Wayne, is you have the evidence and no government to give it to. There are too many corrupt players. If Dunican is dirty, he can't be the only one because a man like that isn't brave enough to do anything alone. It has to be given directly to the people, and without the Internet that will be difficult.

But you have more pressing problems, because the moment you downloaded that footage of my murder, you made yourself traceable, and while our friend Reginald Stanton would most likely tell the government to get fucked if they came calling for that data, under the NET Recovery Act, a federal judge will grant a seizure order within hours. The point being, you need to get the fuck out of Dodge, and as a man with many properties, I'm sure he can keep you hidden until you get it sorted.

Lastly, I know you said the fedora was a gift, but as I won't be using it anymore I'd like you to have it back.

Besides, as you said, anyone who wears that hat can be the Messiah, and there's still work to be done.

Margo, I've worked with some wonderful partners over the years, but you were my favorite. In another life, if your reincarnation isn't still with that asshole Gladstone, I would very much like to open a detective agency with you. Be well, and good luck with Prague Rock Productions.

Gladstone, I'll keep it simple. Thank you for putting me in touch with the subversive, but thank you more for believing in me. I believe in you too.

Sincerely,
Aaron N. Rowsdower

P.S. I've included one more page for the reports. A prologue. I know that's something more fitting for a book than an investigation, but what can I say, you're a terrible influence.

We went from the car to Stanton's helicopter in L.A. to the roof of his Vegas apartment building. I was surprised a helicopter could make a trip that far, but Stanton said that was because I was a "fuckin' drongo." His cowboy yelps, harsh turns, and periodic dives were a good distraction from our grief, and when he finally leveled out and settled into the main leg of the journey, I had a few hours to contemplate the next steps.

Meanwhile, Margo was on her laptop reading through all the evidence that Anonymous had pulled on Hamilton. In some cases, there were paper trails, payments to overseas accounts, contact with known mercenaries, even photos of him and Neville together, picked up by London security street cameras.

When we landed on Stanton's roof, he checked his watch and shouted, "Three thirty! Not bad." He showed all of us the time, pointing to his watch. "And I wasn't even wearing my flight suit," he said. We took the elevator down from the roof to his place on the top floor. It looked a lot like Rowsdower's description of Stanton's place in Manly, except the giant windows now overlooked the Vegas strip. He could have lit his whole place indirectly with the city's sparkle. Margo and I sat in two of the leopard-print recliners facing the bar, and Stanton set out three glasses as he assumed his favorite role of bartender.

"So what'll it be then?" he asked

Margo ordered a Koala Fucker, knowing there wasn't much of a choice.

Stanton took a quick look behind the bar and said, "Ooh, sorry, love. Can't. I'm out of Krazy Straws."

"Ah, I'll just take a vodka soda then if you've got it," she replied.

"Me too," I said. "Minus the vodka."

"On the wagon?" Stanton asked.

"No, but I'm saving it for the right occasion."

Stanton fixed our drinks while he called his messenger service from his landline. "Fuck!" he screamed. "The fuck I will!" He poured himself nearly a full glass of Beauté du Siècle by Hennessey and stared at it with near disdain. "Bullshit!" he yelled. "How'd they do that without me?" He took a gulp. "Yeah? Until when?" Then he paused for a moment before adding, "Fuck," and hanging up.

He brought Margo her drink and said, "They've shut down the Internet again. Not at the hubs. They've rebooted the security protocols, de-verifying those three sites and my PeepHole app. And the government also wants the GPS download data from Rowsdower's broadcast."

"So that means that Dunican told Burke about Rowsdower. And Burke contacted Bhattacharyya or whatever other source he's got in the government."

"Would seem so," Stanton said.

"Well, in fairness to the government," Margo said, "regarding the download data, whoever found out about a former NSA agent's broadcast allegedly involving information about the Internet Apocalypse might want to know more about it for the right reasons."

"Or they just might want to kill whoever downloaded it," Stanton said, topping off his drink.

"Yes, that too," Margo agreed.

"So fuck them. They'll have to seize my operation before I cooperate."

"First of all," I said, "they *will* seize it. Rowsdower's already told us that. But more importantly, I want you to cooperate."

"See?" Stanton said, turning to Margo. "Not leading-man material."

"It's the right play," I explained.

"The fuck it is," Stanton said. "I did not go into business to become a spy for the government. My customers have to know that not every electronic thought or action can become the property of the US government. So why would I give them the GPS data telling them your whereabouts willingly?"

"Because we're no longer in California, so that's a good place to send them looking. And more importantly, you're hiding us so the more they trust you the better off we are. But most of all, because I still need you as a trusted crypto officer. By the way, how did they change the protocols without you? I thought you needed three?"

"Yeah, me too, but my service told me ICANN can use two out of three in an emergency and no one could reach me. Probably because I've been in the sky for the last several hours. I'm calling Leonards to find out more." Stanton checked his iPhone, which, without the Internet, had basically become a Rolodex, and then called from his landline, apparently getting an answering machine. "Kev, it's Reggie. You mind telling me how you and Bhattawhatever rebooted the protocols without me and fucked my app in the process? Call me at my Vegas number. I'll be here."

"Let me ask you this," I said after he hung up. "How would you go about using a key that added all the sites back? Would you need all three crypto officers for that?"

"Well, the code for each new key is reviewed in a ceremony of about twenty wonks. Each is given a handout and we do it line by line on an overhead projector."

"Right, and what happens to that key?" I asked.

"Well, pre-Apocalypse, it was kept in a safe that three crypto officers have access to in case it's needed to reboot the Internet's safety protocols. But now that we're changing protocols weekly, we reboot, allowing in new sites, and then keep it locked up for safekeeping until the next launch that verifies and adds more sites."

For all his swearing and swagger, Stanton's discipline was becoming more clear. Still, I didn't have the information I needed. "Yeah, but what if you went through the ceremony but just used a different key at the end. One that put everything back online?"

"Well, unless all three officers were in on it, someone would notice the switch, but other than that, it could be done."

"Wait a second," Margo said. "Are you fucking kidding me? At ICANN—this international organization with multiple security protocols—in *that* ICANN, three dudes can just decide to use the wrong key and that's that?"

Stanton laughed. "I didn't say it could be done with impunity, but yes it could be done. You'd be shocked to see how much of the world, especially at the highest level of society's structures, is held together by inertia." He finished half his drink in one gulp. "Look," he continued, "the key is generated and placed in a safe. Three trusted crypto officers are given the keys to safety-deposit boxes that contain the cards that, if inserted one right after the other, open the safe to the key card that reboots the security protocols, got me?"

"OK . . ." Margo said.

"But let's say the entire facility is blown up. What then? Well, then there are nine recovery-key shareholders who have a fraction of the security key such that when they come together can rebuild the security key."

"Yes . . ." Margo said, growing impatient.

"But in the event of some catastrophic event where the crypto officers can't get to El Segundo to open the safe and the recovery-key shareholders aren't available to rebuild the key, do you know what the ICANN protocol is then?"

"What?"

"Drill the safe for the fucking key."

"You're shitting me," Margo said.

"I'm not. At the end of the day, it still comes down to sticking a key in a slot, but yeah, one of the three crypto officers would notice any shenanigans and, of course, once the whole Internet came back online it would become pretty obvious what had been done."

"How long to shut it down again?" I asked.

"Well, to realize what had happened, regenerate the right card if it's been destroyed, reboot that, that could buy you some time, but of course the government still controls the hubs, so if they really wanted to shut it down, we're talking minutes. Ten minutes?"

"What are you figuring out?" Margo asked me.

"Not a lot," I said. "Just what I can do in ten minutes that will both destroy Burke and keep the government from pulling the plug on a restored Internet."

"Not following, mate," Stanton said.

"It's like Rowsdower said. We have the evidence, but no government we can trust to give it to. So we give it directly to the people. Make it seen by so many eyes that it can't be unseen. Give the truth to so many people that it can't be taken away."

"How?" Margo asked.

"Well, I'm thinking of a place where the greatest number of people can watch one thing, so . . ."

"Hollywood Bowl?" Margo said.

"Sydney Opera House?" Stanton offered.

"No, I was thinking Times Square. Like with the ball drop on New Year's Eve?"

"Our places definitely hold more people," Margo said.

"Yeah, but unlike your suggestions, walking in New York City is free, just like the Internet we want to return. I also want to hit Burke in his hometown. I think Rowsdower would like that."

"So, what, you want to run some sort of an ad on the Jumbotron screen?" Stanton asked.

"First of all, I want it on *all* the Times Square screens, and not an ad. I'm going to talk to the people. A broadcast on your PeepHole app. I want everyone on their phones watching me, and I want all the evidence Burke collected on the screens all around me."

"But if you do a PeepHole broadcast, you'll reveal your location," Margo said.

"Right, but it's hard to find one man in a packed Times Square. Even harder if he's wearing a hat and holding a phone over his face like everyone else in the crowd."

Margo wasn't happy. Months earlier, she'd found me nearly in pieces, and though I wouldn't say she nursed me, she did watch me. And being watched made it easier to heal and grow, like a plant that's been moved into the sunlight. As I became more of myself, she did too, and then we watched each other—not out of concern but because we liked seeing us become a couple. But now that I was feeling better and more certain than I had in years, Margo was scared.

"They'll kill you," she said.

"Who?" I asked.

"Pick 'em," she said. "There are so many people we can't trust, you can't even take evidence to the government."

"They'd have to kill everyone in that crowd to get to me. I'll be faceless."

"Well, none of this means anything if Crypto Dundee here can't get the Net rebooted anyway."

"Crypto Dundee?" Stanton asked.

"Sorry. That was stupid," Margo said. "I'm upset."

Stanton's phone rang, and he was pleased to see it was Leonards returning his call. "Kevin, thanks for . . . Well, I'm in Vegas, aren't I?" Stanton switched into listening mode as best he could. "What do you mean confession, this isn't . . . Oh . . . oh, I'm sorry to hear that. . . . That bad, huh? Rough. . . . So Friday's still on then? Tell him to hold on, Kevin. I'm coming to get you. Both of you . . . yeah, well, you tell him I know a way out of hell."

Stanton put down the phone and finished the rest of his drink. "Well, I think rebooting the Internet just got a lot easier. Neville confessed to Leonards. Rowsdower and Anonymous were right: Neville was Burke's mole. Also, he's dying."

Stanton went to his hall closet and pulled out a flight jumpsuit. "You guys get some sleep, I'll be back tomorrow with Leonards and Neville."

"One second," Margo said. "You can't let him know where we are. He might be lying."

"How the hell do you think I became a multibillionaire?" Stanton asked. "I'm aware of that possibility, and aside from having a fairly good bullshit detector, I'm also gonna run him by Jeeves."

"Jeeves is still in L.A.?" I asked.

"Yeah, he's staying in my pool house. One of the perks of being on staff. That guy picks stocks like a motherfucker . . . well, after meeting the CEOs of certain companies at a little party I threw the other night."

"Isn't that insider trading?" Margo asked.

"Sort of?" Stanton replied. "But I'm pretty sure there's nothing about psychics in SEC regulations. Besides, is that really your biggest problem now? Anyway, if it all checks out, I'll have Leonards and Neville here tomorrow and we'll figure it out."

"You can't fly yet," I said. "You've been drinking."

"Why do you think I'm putting on my *Airwolf* flight suit? If I'm going to wait an hour to sober up, I gotta make some time."

I woke at around eight the next morning, but Margo was already working on her Mac at Stanton's bedroom desk. She was wearing nothing but her underwear and my corduroy sports jacket. One of her long legs disappeared under the desk while the other stretched out to her right.

The master bedroom, where we'd decided to sleep, featured a bed far bigger than "king" and a giant Andy Warhol print of our host over the headboard. There was also a bearskin rug on the floor and a stuffed koala clutching a fake eucalyptus tree in the corner. It seemed extreme wealth was just as damaging to sanity as poverty.

"Whatcha working on?" I asked, but Margo was too studious to be distracted by me. I got out of bed and put my arms around her middle, nuzzling my chin into her neck. I could see she was tweaking the data Anonymous had collected on Burke, turning it into an animated PowerPoint. The images and documents came up in quick succession one after another, tying Burke to hit men and terrorists, and she had the whole thing on a loop.

"I wanted to get it to a repeated five minutes," she said. "Enough information to make an impact and to be recorded by anyone filming the screen."

"You're so talented, baby," I said.

"Now, let's work on your speech," she said.

"Don't worry," I said, "I got it."

"That confident?" she asked.

"Well, the last time I wrote something," I replied, "this super foxy L.A. chick optioned it for a movie."

"So I assume you'll be wearing your grandfather's fedora?" she asked.

"Yes," I answered.

"So you don't mind if I wear the Bowie one?" It was already on the desk and she put it on. It slid down slightly and bent her ears. She looked up at me from under the brim with big doe eyes.

"Not at all," I said. "Makes sense."

She frowned and took the hat off, laying it back on the desk.

"What?" I asked.

"You didn't even say I looked cute," she said in a deliberately pouty voice.

"Oh, baby, I'm sorry," I said. "You're adorable." I put the hat back on her and gave her a kiss.

"Jerk," she said, milking the offense in a way she rarely did.

"I'm sorry, Margo," I said. "You're my best friend. Sometimes I just forget you're a girl."

"It's OK, Gladstone," she said. "Sometimes I forget that about you too."

Stanton returned with Leonards and Neville a few hours later. I'd never met Neville, but he looked sicker than Rowsdower had described in his reports. His arm was around Leonards, an older but stronger man, who brought him to the leopard-print couch in the living room—the one behind the leopard-print recliners. And once the professor made sure Neville was planted, he turned to me with real joy.

"Gladdy," he said. "I'm so happy you're well." And even though I'd only met him once, he hugged me like an old friend. I'd read Rowsdower's report. I knew Leonards was a rebel and that he approved of what I'd started, or what had been started around me, but surely part of what I was feeling was more.

"Rowsdower's dead," I said, and his joy turned more serious than sad.

"I know," he said. "Reggie's told us everything, but we're gonna make it right, aren't we?"

"I hope so."

"Good news, lads," Stanton interrupted, brandishing Krazy Straws. "I stopped at Ralphs before we came back. Koala Fuckers all around."

Stanton went to the bar and Margo and I pulled the recliners around to face Neville and Leonards on the couch.

"I did it," Neville said to me before breaking into a hacking cough. He pulled a handkerchief from the silk pajamas he was wearing and even though he wiped his face like an elegant English gentleman, I could see there was blood in it. I could also see what was left of his hair shedding. "I know you know, but I wanted to say it to you. I helped Hamilton."

"For money?" I asked.

"For a lot of money," he replied. "My business had failed, and I had three children to take care of."

"Surely they wouldn't have starved," I said.

"No, but I can tell you as someone who's seen both, it's a lot harder to stop being rich than only to live poor." He turned to Margo. "Hello, Ms. Zmena. Nice to see you again."

"Hello, Mr. Bhattacharyya," she said. "You've taken quite the turn. . . ."

"I've started chemo," he said. "I was gonna just, y'know, die, but I've decided to fight it. Yesterday I was recovering from my second round of chemo, and you know what? They called me. They pulled me out of Cedars-Sinai and brought me to El Segundo to reboot their bloody protocols again because of Rowsdower's PeepHole broadcast, and that's when I realized I can't die like this. I want my children to be proud of me."

"Really?" I said. "I thought you just wanted to make sure they didn't have to come home from Exeter or summer someplace more pedestrian than San Tropez?"

"Wayne," Margo said.

"Wayne what? I'm not sure what this guy wants." I leaned in to Neville. "You want me to bless you? I'm not that kind of messiah. You want me to say it's all OK? It's not OK. You're part of the problem. You're dying of cancer in silk pajamas because you smoke and because you had the ill-gotten money to buy fucking silk pajamas. I'm sorry. I know you're not supposed to speak ill of the dead, but this is my first chance as I've only just met you. Also, you're still kicking."

"OK, Gladstone," Stanton said from the bar.

"No, it sure as hell is not OK. My friend Rowsdower is dead. He's dead for doing the right thing. He's dead because he believed in me and what I'm doing. He was good and he's dead, and the world is a worse place because he's gone. You? You're some rich chain-smoking English prick who wants to die feeling like a good guy after selling out the world to a murderer."

"I didn't know there'd be murder," Neville said. "I just thought he was playing some moneymaking angle. I didn't know, and I'm sorry Rowsdower is dead, but I need to ask you something. Is your dollar-store story true?"

"Yes," I said. "It's true. They were the happiest little girls in the world. For three dollars, their father was a hero. They loved him."

"Do you think they always did?" Neville asked.

"I don't know. Those little girls are all adults now, but what does that matter? It's not about what happened after that; it's about what can happen. He was a hero, even if just for that day. Even if those kids were taken by the state due to neglect ten years later. Even if they all became crack whores dying of HIV from shared needles. Even then, I'm guessing that before their malnourished, syphilitic bodies fell to dust on a clinic bed someone told them to think back to their happiest memory as the morphine filled their veins. And I truly believe, even under the worst of circumstances, they'd think back to that day. They'd have that day to remember. And that is what I believe in. I believe in that day."

Stanton coughed again. "I thought you believed in pure things?" he said.

"Sometimes, one day is all the purity we get," I said.

"What are you going to do with your one day, Mr. Bhattacharyya?"

He returned his handkerchief to his pocket and said, "Stanton told me the plan. Professor Leonards and I are perfectly capable of crafting a new DNSSEC protocol to let all the sites back, and I will be the one to insert it. They can deny knowledge. I will take the fall, but you have to tell me your plan will destroy Burke. Because now I know he's a murderer, and even when I'm gone my children won't be."

"I will do everything I can to destroy him. No one, Mr. Bhattacharyya, no one wants him dead more than I." Neville nodded. "But there's something I want from you first," I said.

"What's that?"

I took out the phone Rowsdower had given me and flipped on the video recorder. "A confession. Documents are one thing, but turning state's evidence is another."

He sat up as best he could and ran his hand back through his shedding hair. "OK, Mr. Gladstone," he said. "I'm ready."

"Thank you, Neville. Of course, this all means nothing unless I can get in touch with Anonymous and make sure they can hack the Times Square screens."

"Oh, right, about that," Stanton said. "I called Jeeves's place from Neville's and spoke to Tobey. Anonymous is still holding their meetups with 4chan on Tuesday nights. So once you're done with your shoot, we better get you to New York."

Days 437–440

The next morning, Stanton flew Margo and me to New York in his private jet, which he piloted himself. That was good, because the bottle of booze I stole from his bar—his best—didn't present a security problem on his plane. Margo and I had decided to stay at a centrally located hotel called the Mansfield, which wasn't too far from Times Square or the New York Public Library.

Over the next few days, we pretended the room was our apartment. It didn't feel like an apartment, and in truth it wasn't even the greatest of rooms, but we were days away from finishing what I'd accidentally started, and having a home felt like a necessity. I needed to recharge and prepare for the Internet's return so I could make my pitch to keep it there. But there was another reason. After Friday, everything could change. It could be worse. It could be over. These few nights could be my last chance to hold Margo all through the night, to look out from a window in the sky and care more about the person beside me than all of New York City.

The meeting with Anonymous on Tuesday night went better than I could have hoped. We sat in the audience and no one noticed us. Why would they? Margo had dressed as Oz, applying some intense winged eye makeup, and wearing a bright blue wig. I wore a Gladstone mask, which turned out to be the most popular costume at the meetup. They were popping up everywhere. Not just bookstores and Starbucks (who also sold their own copy of my book) but even in Times Square tourist shops and from the kind of street vendors who sell Statue of Liberty foam visors. She'd been licensing like a champ.

Margo confirmed for me that the man leading that night's meeting was the Black Fawkes Down guy Rowsdower trusted, although, not being a moron, she didn't call him that. Tobey (who was dressed as Tobey with no mask) had reestablished himself at 4chan, so after the show was over he was able to get us backstage for a private meeting. That was good because I didn't want to announce my identity to a roomful of strangers.

We didn't speak at first. Instead, Margo took out her Mac and played the presentation she'd made, showing Rowsdower's murder followed by a flow of the Hamilton Burke–incriminating evidence Anonymous had gathered while Fawkes sat on the same old ratty green room couch I'd seen before.

"Well done," Fawkes said.

"Did you know Burke was Quiffmonster?" I asked.

"I'd suspected it for some time. If you notice, he's not

around here anymore. He stopped appearing after he started running for president."

"Well, y'know the damage is already done," I said.

"I'm sorry, Gladstone," he replied, and I took off my Gladstone mask because, really, what was the point?

"Don't be. It's not your fault, and thank you for helping us gather this information. . . ." I paused. "I'm sorry I don't even know your fake name."

"Most people here just call me Black Fawkes," he said.

"Really?" Tobey asked. "I thought that was just me."

"Well, actually, it is mostly just you, but that's the closest I have to a pseudonym."

"How about Black Fawkes Down," I suggested.

"Pass," he said.

"Too racist?" I asked.

"Too stupid. Anyway, you're welcome."

I explained to Black Fawkes that while I trusted him, I didn't want anyone else to know I was in town. I also explained everything we wanted to achieve for Friday. A massive Times Square demonstration timed with ICANN's return of the Internet. We wanted to create an event that could be witnessed, downloaded, and spread around, before the government shut the Net down at the hubs or, better yet, until the government realized that so many people were mobilized that it *couldn't* be shut down.

Margo clarified the point from a PR perspective. "So keeping Gladstone's presence a secret isn't just for security reasons," she said. "It's the whole angle for the presentation. We're building anticipation for the event: This Friday, the Internet Messiah Comes Home. That's the word we're spreading and we want you to spread."

"That is not a problem," he said.

"Right, but now the harder part," I interrupted. "We need Anonymous to hack all the Jumbotron screens in Times Square to play this video on a loop starting at noon while I'm doing a PeepHole broadcast. And at some point, to directly broadcast my PeepHole broadcast from the screens."

"That is also no problem," he said.

"This is important," Margo said. "It's no time for bravado."

"It's not bravado," he insisted. "We already know how to do that. We've been planning the prank for weeks. We were gonna run a Photoshop of Obama and Senator Melissa Bramson having sex, but your idea is much better."

"Thanks," I said.

"Well, maybe you can include the Photoshop at the end too," Tobey suggested. "Win-win."

"Thank you, Fawkes," I said, ignoring Tobey, and placed a flash drive containing the presentation in his hand. This Friday at noon."

"Anonymous is with you, Gladstone."

"I've been burned by you before," I said.

"Gladstone, I read the book. You've been burned by everything," he said, "But you're still here, and I will do my best, as well as anyone can do, to make sure we get the right collaborators. And to that end, maybe you should go out the back way, it's—"

"I got this," I said, remembering my last 4chan escape from more than a year before, and pulled open the closet door. A naked man in a Nixon mask, who had clearly been masturbating in the closet, fell wanking to the floor. Hentai porn prints spilled out everywhere.

"Goddammit, Glendoria4," Fawkes shouted. "How many fucking times!"

And so I sat in a New York hotel room, a guest in my own city with a woman from L.A. Nowhere left to go and no place I'd rather be. Stanton had sent a fax from L.A. to the Mansfield Thursday night. Attention: Parker Lawrence. Everything was on for Friday. All I had to do was make this last night feel more like home, like pulling up the covers tight after you're already in bed.

That night I held Margo while we watched TV. The rumors had spread. The people were going to gather. No permit had been obtained, but no specific presentation had been promised and no violence was expected. All everyone knew was that they should bring a fedora, sports jacket, and phone because Gladstone was coming home.

"I love you, Wayne," she said.

"I've almost gotten used to you calling me Parker."

"I like calling you Parker," she said, "But for now, I wanted to make sure you knew I had the right guy."

I smiled and tucked her hair behind her ear. "I love you so much, Margo, that even if I hated your fucking guts, I'd still want to spend every single day with you."

She laughed, and I asked, "Do you understand?"

"I totally understand," she said. "I hate you too."

I reached over to the bedside lamp, making sure to keep Margo on my chest, and shut off the light.

We had a very late breakfast in the morning and then walked out separately to Times Square. I needed to do this alone, and if bullets were to start flying, I didn't want

Margo anywhere near me. The crowd wasn't quite New Year's Eve, you could still move and walk, but about 75 percent of the people were wearing sports jackets and fedoras, or even better, Gladstone masks. Margo was somewhere in this crowd of everyday people, but she was wearing a $2,000 sports jacket she'd stolen from Stanton's closet and a hat that once belonged to David Bowie.

The time on my iPhone read 11:55 and I worked my way to that riser in the center of Times Square beneath the biggest of the many giant screens. As a child, waiting for Broadway show tickets with my mom and dad on Christmas, Times Square was skyscrapers and one giant movie screen. Now it was a bunch of televisions stapled to buildings, but it was still the best place I could think of, and I hoped hijacking twenty TVs would have the same impact as holding one movie screen hostage.

At 11:58, Margo's presentation started playing on every single screen in Times Square. Silent, but explosive. It started with a simple message: "Gladstone and the Internet will be here in moments." All the Gladstones in the crowd started pointing and looking among them. The next message flashed: "Get ready to download the PeepHole app. Follow WGladstone." Most of the crowd probably already had the app on their phones, considering PeepHole's downloads had shattered all records the week before with the advantage of being the only app available during the Apocalypse. Still, a heads-up couldn't hurt, and I'm sure Stanton appreciated the financial reward of being a revolutionary. Unfortunately, my username was "WGladstone" because even in the Apocalypse, I wasn't the first one to try to register "Gladstone."

At noon, the screens all changed again: "THE INTER-NET IS BACK!!!" I opened up my Gmail and sent a test to myself. It went through. Anonymous had hacked the screens, the ICANN crypto officers had staged a revolt, and now it was up to me to keep it going. I opened my PeepHole app and hit Broadcast, holding my phone in front of my face on the highest step of the riser. I was online, but I waited. I wanted to give everyone a chance to follow me, to find me, to realize they were connected and able to listen. And after another two minutes, I looked out into a crowd of sports jackets and fedoras and saw a phone where nearly every face should have been. And I laughed because those with iPhones had apples in front of their faces like living re-creations of Magritte's *Son of Man*.

"Hello from the Internet," I said, and even though the sound came out of my mouth I heard it everywhere. It was coming out of all the phones in Times Square, bouncing from the M&M building to Ernst & Young, like speaking into a powerful microphone. I checked the screens to make sure the presentation had changed to Rowsdower's footage.

"My name is Wayne Gladstone," I said, and I had to stop there because the crowd erupted into cheers. "Thank you, but our time may be limited," I said. "On all these screens around me you will see Former Special Agent Aaron N. Rowsdower being murdered by his NSA boss, Patrick Dunican. I know many of you know Rowsdower from my journal, where I was kind of a dick to him, but he was a good man. He was my friend. He helped me. And his teeth were totally normal, by the way. Anyway, he fought to bring the Internet back to all of you, and he was murdered. That name again is Patrick Dunican, but

Dunican was killing for another. On behalf of the same man who murdered my ex-wife, Romaya Petralia, and ICANN crypto officer Michiko Nagasoto. On behalf of the man behind so many of these bombings. The same man who took the Internet from us in the first place. Special Agent Rowsdower was murdered trying to give evidence to the government. So today, I give that evidence to you. All of you here today must bear witness to the evidence Rowsdower tried to share in vain."

I waited for Rowsdower's footage to finish playing, blood dripping from his forced smile. "The man behind the Apocalypse, the terrorism, the murder, is Hamilton Burke." The screens filled with Burke's image, and I could tell by the reaction that the crowd didn't want to believe. "Anonymous has gathered the records," I said. "Look carefully and you will see a paper trail tying Burke to murder and terrorism." The incriminating documents flashed by one by one, finally resting on an image of Hamilton with Neville. Faces peeked out from behind phones. It was too dense for them. Too many words. And too much not about the Internet.

"Switch to me," I said. It was a message to Anonymous and suddenly every single screen in Times Square was transmitting my PeepHole broadcast, and everyone had the audio from their phones to match with the images on the big screen. I took out Margo's phone, where I'd transferred Bhattacharyya's confession and hit Play, holding her phone in front of mine. Times Square was now filled with Neville, a sick Indian Englishman, confessing almost from the grave.

"My name is Neville Bhattacharyya," he said. "Tech Global founder, ICANN crypto officer, and, to my dishonor, willing collaborator with Hamilton Burke. I was one of the many people in power collaborating to provide gaps in the Internet's security protocols that allowed Hamilton Burke to stage cyberattacks. I am sorry. But I must also stress that after those attacks, it was the United States government who shut down the Internet. First at the hubs, turning it off like a switch, but even when it returned, they metered it out, bit by bit, pursuant to their directives and inclinations. One monster's tantrum became an excuse for the systemic restriction of a public commodity. Please do not forget that as we move forward. But if all goes as planned, today the Internet will be returned to you, and I hope it remains. Good luck."

I put Margo's phone back in my pocket and checked my watch. The Internet had been on for six minutes. "We're still broadcasting," I said, and the crowd cheered. The same cheers I'd heard them give Hamilton. The cheers of people who had what they wanted. Good people, bad people, but all satisfied.

"In our current climate, I'm not sure everyone who had a part in this would want me to identify them by name, but I didn't do this myself. It took an army. And not just an army of soldiers like Rowsdower, but an army of believers, businesspeople, and fools."

That didn't get much of a response, but I only said it for my friends anyway. Tobey and Margo were somewhere out there in that crowd, and Jeeves, Leonards, and Stanton were listening in. "Y'know, about a year ago," I continued, "I said I wasn't the Messiah. That anyone wearing the hat could be the Messiah. And in that way, we all did this today, so thank you!"

The crowd cheered again, and that was good, because now I was really going to lose them. I lowered my phone so I could peek out between its top and the brim of my hat. There could be hit men at any one of the literally hundreds of windows around me. But what would be the point of killing me now? The information was out there.

"Before I go," I said, "I did want to tell you one more thing. This army we put together that pulled the Internet back from the hands of tyrants is not undefeated. When it comes to the Internet, we are always vulnerable."

Even though my voice was still bouncing off every Times Square surface, it started to sound thin, unaccepted by an audience, and rattling until it fell like unwanted change on a dirty floor.

"The Internet connects us to everything, but if we're not careful, we still see the whole of the world through a peephole. A tiny crack of our own design. We joke that we put filters on our Instagram pictures to make ourselves more beautiful to the world, but it works in reverse too. We filter what we take in. The Internet gives us unfettered power to control how we see the world. What information we receive. And like anyone with that kind of power and control, there comes the expectation of comfort. This is the new normal, the belief that we should not be challenged. That things should not make us uncomfortable. But some things are supposed to make us uncomfortable."

I had a good ten seconds before everyone stopped listening, and it occurred to me you could lose an audience quicker than the government could cut an Internet connection.

"Look, I understand the importance of safe spaces," I said. "I just spent the last six months hiding in an Australian mine because I'd lost everything I'd ever had and loved. It felt good to stay someplace where I had full control of what I let into my world, but if I stayed there, I never would have been able to build a life with the woman I love. I never would have seen my friends again. I never would have been with you here today. I know some of you don't want to hear this, but that's sort of the point. Soon, you'll download all your other apps and watch something else."

I was no longer the only voice. I'd started a murmur in the audience, perhaps by introducing the idea that there were other things to be watching.

"I'm in the middle of Times Square with all of you. And I'm sure some of you are absolute assholes and some of you are cruel and some of you are scared. You are victims and abusers and beggars and kings and I want to see all of you. And I want you to see me. One second," I said.

I took off my coat and put it by my feet and then I took off my hat. I was exposed. I was shouting. "My name is Wayne Gladstone, and I'm home. This is my face. Show me yours. Throw off your hats. Lift up your phones. Gimme your hands. You're wonderful!"

The hats flew like a graduation ceremony, and when they fell, I started shouting because I was holding the phone farther from my face, my other arm flapping wildly. "I'm here. I'm the asshole on the riser, waving. Take your shot. Are you a government operative? Are you a hit man for Hamilton Burke? Go for it. We know everything now. You won't get paid. You won't advance your career. You've been seen."

The crowd returned to their prior stillness. After all, seeing me take a bullet would be the most epic of fails for an audience that hadn't seen a YouTube humiliation for more than a year. They waited for me to fall and bleed, but I didn't fall. I didn't bleed. And after a moment I reached down and put my hat and jacket back on. "Yeah, that's what I thought," I said, and everyone started jumping again.

"There's one more thing I have to do before I go," I said. "Hamilton?" I asked. "You listening? Because this last part's for you." I brought the phone tight to my face and looked directly into the lens. "It's over. You're going to have to hide now, Hamilton. I know. I've been there. And I'm sorry. Unlike me who got to hide when the world went dark, we're online now. We've returned what you took away, and that's going to make your hiding all the more difficult.

"It's sort of like when you turn a computer on in the dark. You ever do that? And suddenly a little tiny bug lands on the screen. You discover you'd been living with an insect and you never realized until it was drawn to the light. That bug's a lot like you, Hamilton, because staying hidden isn't in your nature. You're the kind of man who needs to stamp his name on things. To own things. You need eyes on you or you cease to exist.

"Anyway, Hamilton, I have to go get arrested for criminal mischief if I remember my Crim Law from school, and you have to figure out how to end your existence. But before you go, I wanted to let you know I've been on the wagon for the last few months. I've been waiting for a special occasion."

The flask with the booze from Stanton's bar was inside

my coat pocket, nestled with my old love letter to Romaya where the two had lived side by side for so long. And when I pulled the flask out, the letter came with it, catching the wind as if it had been waiting for its very first opportunity to be free. I watched it disappear into the Times Square crowd. It was gone.

"Hamilton," I said. "I have here a flask of Beauté du Siècle by Hennessey, your brand if I remember correctly. Here's to you, Hamilton. Goodbye." I took a deep swig and returned the flask to my pocket. "Thank you all," I said, "And remember, we need the evidence, so now's a good time to hit Download, and if anyone does try to shut the Internet down again, well, then it's up to all of you. Carry the news."

Dear Wayne,

It's only been an hour since I left. One hour since I watched them lead you back to your cell, and you snuck that last peek over your shoulder to see me crying behind the glass.

I don't want you to worry. I wasn't sad. I know I'll see you soon. (Three to six months is soon, right?) I cried because even handcuffed and wearing prison clothes, I could see you were stronger than when we first met. You were more you. And with you, I am more me. This is what we do for each other.

I love you,
Margo

P.S. This is my only copy of this letter, and now it's yours.

Acknowledgments

First, I would like to thank my editor, Peter Joseph, who had faith in this trilogy before it even existed. If not for Peter's request for an epilogue in Book Two, Special Agent Rowsdower may have never ended up being the narrator of Book Three. Sometimes good things come from a tiny, thoughtful suggestion. I also want to thank my agent, Lauren Abramo, who navigated me through this entire process start to finish, dealing with a Gladstone who was a lot more sober, focused, and generally irritating than the Gladstone of these novels.

The nice thing about writing a trilogy is that it gives you three chances to get something right, so I want to acknowledge some of the people I failed to mention, or mention sufficiently, earlier.

Music played an incredibly important role in these novels. Book One was composed almost entirely to Arcade Fire's *The Suburbs* and Interpol's fourth album. The soundtrack for Book Two was ELO's *New World Record* and, to help me get into an Internet-less L.A. mindset, Don Henley's "Boys of Summer" and "Sunset Grill." I struggled to find a matching soundtrack in the early parts of Book Three. I revisited all the past recordings mentioned above and threw in some Crowded House and Beck with limited results. And then David Bowie's *Blackstar* came out, and then he died.

I can't really articulate what Bowie's death meant to me. I had always found mourning celebrities somewhat false and foolish, but the impact was undeniable. I stopped writing the novel for a few days, and I was very lucky that during that time, Rick Moody reached out to me and asked if I would trade emails with him about Bowie's final album and demise. Sure, it was an honor to write anything with a great novelist like Rick, but I was touched more by the belief that he was looking out for me. That he gave me a chance to grieve through writing, and I am very grateful.

I then immersed myself in the book, Bowie, and *Blackstar,* writing the second half of the novel faster than I'd ever written before. Bowie is everywhere in this book, and for a story that's largely about learning to be brave, I think that's as it should be.

Also on the list of people who did not get proper thanks, I must mention my friend Liz Coleman, who is best described as the benefactor of this trilogy. Over the last few years, Liz has done so many small favors to help this universe exist: keeping facts in her head to remind me about forgotten details, coming up with theories that I found illuminating and/or infuriating, and even proofreading drafts. It was invaluable. Also, she taught me to speak Australian and even shot video on the ferry to Manly. Thank you, Liz.

Also great thanks and apologies to my friend (and sometimes Styks & Stones podcast cohost) Maura Chwastyk, who was on the receiving end of far too many plot scenario generations. As I spewed permutations over and over, looking for a pattern that fit, Maura always knew when to give me feedback and when to just let me clatter on. I don't think I would have figured it out without her.

And speaking of Australians, big thanks to C. Coville and Tomas Fitzgerald for additional details used in Gladstone's time abroad.

Thanks to my friends Brendan McGinley and Matt Tobey for lending their names to "Brendan Tobey." It should also be noted that Matt Tobey is even better at "Six Degrees of Stanley Tucci" than his fictional counterpart.

Thanks also to Andrew Blum for his wonderful book, *Tubes*, essential reading for anyone fascinated with the Internet. Thank you to copy editor extraordinaire Rachelle Mandik, who aside from finding all my errors, was good enough to let me know important details like, there's only one Andrew's Coffee Shop left in New York.

Lastly, thank you to my entire family, but most of all, the three magical weirdos, Asher, Sage, and Quinn. You are the best of everything, and a trilogy far better than these novels.